Collin opened his eyes and locked on to her in a hypnotic gaze.

Athena moved closer to him, creeping forward until she got to the couch.

His hand reached toward her. She held her breath. Once his fingers touched her cheek and cupped the side of her face, she exhaled. Gently he guided her face to his. Athena's pulse quickened with anticipation for the kiss she could almost taste.

Collin's gaze shifted to her mouth. On cue her lips responded, opening slightly as they touched his, molding along his lips. Athena closed her eyes to savor the moment, for how long could this last?

Time meant nothing. Her lips sparked to life with the feel of his kiss. Every part of her, from the roots of her hair to the tips of her toes, reacted to the new sensation of being awakened.

Sherman

Books by Michelle Monkou

Kimani Romance

Sweet Surrender
Here and Now
Straight to the Heart
No One But You
Gamble on Love
Only in Paradise

Kimani Arabesque

Open Your Heart
Finders Keepers
Give Love
Making Promises
Island Rendezvous

MICHELLE MONKOU

became a world traveler at the age of three when she left her birthplace of London, England, and moved to Guyana, South America. She then moved to the United States as a young teen. Avid reading, mixed with her cultural experiences, set the tone for a vivid imagination. It wasn't long before the stories in her head became stories on paper.

In the middle of writing romances, Michelle added a master's of international business to her bachelor's degree in English. She was nominated for the 2003 Emma Award for Favorite New Author. She continues to write romance novels with complex characters and intricate plots. Visit her Web site for further information, and to sign up for her newsletter and contests, at www.michellemonkou.com.

Having lived on three continents, Michelle currently resides in the Washington, D.C., metropolitan area with her family. To contact her, write to P.O. Box 2904, Laurel, Maryland 20709, or e-mail her at michellemonkou@comcast.net.

Only in PARADISE

Michelle Monkou

KIMANI
ROMANCE

To my own hero, Bryan.
Twenty-five years and counting. I love you.

 KIMANI PRESS™

Recycling programs
for this product may
not exist in your area.

ISBN-13: 978-0-373-86107-1
ISBN-10:   0-373-86107-9

ONLY IN PARADISE

www.kimanipress.com

Printed in U.S.A.

Dear Reader,

Step into the world of Xi Sigma Theta Sorority, Inc. Athena Crawford and her four line sisters from the pledge line—the Ladies of Distinction—have forged a deep friendship. They have shared the trials and tribulations of their college years and now embark on finding their destinies as young professionals. Each soror will share her story of pain, redemption and, ultimately, love.

As a member of Sigma Gamma Rho Sorority, Inc., I wanted to create stories highlighting the tight bond among sorority sisters. African-American fraternal organizations have had a long history of servicing our communities, forming powerful networks and working with our youth. As we cut our affiliation from the few who have negative and hurtful intentions, I look forward to the focused and unified messages from the various Greek organizations in the twenty-first century.

If you are a member of a sorority or enjoy a close-knit group of dear friends, share your positive experiences in building on sisterhood beyond the family. I have had many great friends throughout my life and I look forward to forging more friendships in the future.

Contact me at michellemonkou@comcast.net.

Blessings,

Michelle Monkou

Chapter 1

Athena Crawford fastened her gaze on her hands, which rested in her lap. Thinking about her loss hurt too much. While she grieved, Mother Nature showed no mercy with the cloudless, blue sky and unusually warm September sun streaming its bright beam over the group as if it was a normal day.

There was nothing normal about losing her grandmother.

Behind her dark glasses, Athena only wanted to remember her grandmother's warm, gentle nature. Childhood memories of wonderful summers at her house nestled softly in her heart.

Today, here at the cemetery for the burial, she constantly fought the choking swell of emotion. Her heart ached. She'd willingly plead for more time to spend with her grandma. She didn't care how selfish that was.

Grandma had impacted her teaching career with lasting positive changes. In a different time, she'd kicked open doors that were shut tight.

I wonder if I have that same courage, Athena thought.

Sitting on the little metal folding chair, she had to focus on her hands, her fingers, anything, rather than the dark, cold space that swallowed her grandmother's casket in its cavernous mouth.

Even her sorority, Xi Theta Sigma, earned the benefits of Grandma's wisdom when she pledged at its first chapter in Kansas in 1963. From there, she helped start several local chapters throughout the state, also sharing the principles of the founders, who were all teachers. Always the person to think about giving back to the community, her grandma created a task force of volunteer teachers to go into low-income communities on the weekends to supplement children's regular education.

This week had been laden with various memorials honoring her grandmother's contributions. Now the final home-going service had come too soon.

Athena had also lost her favorite listener. No more would she smell the light floral scent of her grandmother's favorite cologne. Nor would she hear the raspy chortle that conveyed her grandmother's dry sense of humor. Always the lady, her grandmother never stepped outdoors without a stylish hat. Hats were just her thing.

Yet what stood as fact and not only opinion, and reiterated by those in attendance at the funeral service, was her grandmother's astute ability to zero in on a person's need and provide the appropriate wisdom. Gift and skill, Grandma respected that ability and readily dispensed her knowledge, especially to Athena and her twin sister, Asia.

A soft breeze blew in, stroking Athena's cheek like a warm breath. She smoothed a few wayward tendrils of hair behind her ear. Grandma used to fix her stubborn hair while imparting her latest round of advice. Their most pivotal career conversation occurred a couple years before, though it was as easy to recall as yesterday.

"Athena, sweetheart, you can't go through life without passion." Her grandmother drummed her polished nails on the glass dining table, while her gaze locked onto her granddaughter's face.

"I don't have a choice," Athena whined. "This finance job pays the bills." She cleared her throat to get rid of the tears that fought their way to the surface.

"What is this really about? You're not the weepy sort. Is it the job? Relationship with a boyfriend that's gone astray?"

"Grandma!" Athena's cheeks burned. She didn't have a boyfriend, but she didn't expect to talk about her love life with her grandmother. "The problem is that I feel like those pet hamsters that have nothing else to do but run in the wheel. I'm not going anywhere in this job. I don't feel as if I'm learning anything new." Athena took a deep breath. "How did you stay focused? By my age, you'd done so much more than I could ever think to do."

"I grew up in very different times, honey. I didn't want my children to suffer. In my heart I believed that education was the step stone to a better life. And so I wanted to teach."

Athena smiled. "I think that's what I want to do, too." Excitement welled. She leaned forward, resting her elbows on the table.

"I appreciate you wanting to follow in my footsteps. I'm flattered and my heart couldn't be happier. But you have to tap into your own special gift."

Athena nodded. "I have something to show you." Athena went to her pocketbook and pulled out the folded paper. She paused before handing it over.

Her grandmother read the contents. Her hand shook slightly. Then her other hand partially covered her mouth. "You got accepted to grad school in education. You're going to be a teacher." Her brown eyes sparkled, accentuated by the ready, wide smile.

"Why not? I had a good life teacher in you." Athena hugged her grandmother, feeling as if her frail arms transmitted the wisdom and strength of their mutual female ancestors.

Athena pressed her feet in the grass, imagining their prints pressing a new path toward destiny. The breeze continued to wrap her shoulders with its attention. The special memory shared between her grandmother and her would always stay with her.

She was lulled out of her daydream by Asia's voice. "Here're a few more tissues."

Athena took the tissues from Asia, her twin, only just realizing that her tears had increased their flow down her cheeks. A steady blur at her periphery marked the departure of the large number of well-wishers. She wiped her runny nose, and inhaled a shuddering breath.

"Athena, sweetheart, we're going to head back for the repast," her father said. He looked over to her mother, concern etched in his lined face. "I'm planning to take your mom to the Poconos after this. We need to rest." He sighed. "We'll see you and your sister soon."

Athena nodded. She wished that she could be strong enough for him to lean on and help with her mother.

"Mr. Crawford, we'll be there to help out," offered Sara, her sorority sister.

"Thanks, ladies. You know you're like family. We're glad you could come," her father responded.

Then Sara and her other sorority sisters flanked either side of her father and headed over to talk with her mother.

Athena had to admit that she felt comforted by their presence. Their pledge line name—Ladies of Distinction—proved to be an accurate description, time and again.

After her parents drove away, her sorors returned, forming a huddle around Athena and Asia. Sara led the prayer, after which, they each shared a reassuring hug with them.

"I'm going to miss her." Athena dabbed at her nose. "I'm a teacher because of her." She sniffed loudly. "She encouraged me throughout grad school to make it happen."

Asia nodded her silent acknowledgment, wiping a tear from her cheek.

Athena continued, "Third generation in the family to be a teacher, you know."

Her sorority sisters also nodded, although they already knew her personal history.

"She was a good, special soul, soror." Sara put her arm around Athena's shoulders and provided a comforting hug. Her cheek cushioned Athena's head that rested in place.

Naomi's tall, athletic frame moved into view. "Can we continue this at Athena's place?" Naomi glanced out over the cemetery. She rubbed her arms to emphasize her discomfort with a noisy shudder. "Besides, the sun is setting." She squinted toward the horizon.

"What's your problem? Maybe Athena isn't ready," Asia stated. Her tone didn't hold back the warning to Naomi to back off from her sister.

"What's the hurry? It's off-season. And you don't have any basketball games, Miss Celebrity," Denise piped up with the tilt of her head toward Asia.

"I know you don't have a darn place to get to." Sara scowled at Naomi, waving her off.

"Enough with the attack! I'm just saying that we may want to think about leaving." Naomi threw up her hand, clearly frustrated. "Nightfall and a cemetery don't go together." Naomi paced back and forth in front of the group. "It's creepy…too quiet." She paused to look out over the cemetery. "But some might not be resting, if you catch my drift." Again she rubbed her arms a little longer than necessary, considering the moderate temperature. "We shouldn't be among…

them." She looked over her shoulder, causing Sara, Asia and Denise to crane their necks in the same direction.

Despite her teary sniffles, Athena couldn't help a small chuckle at Naomi's over-the-top fear. Even her soror's microbraids flitted around her head as if they were alive and also panicked.

"You're such a ditz," Denise finally declared. "How'd you manage to stay overnight in a cemetery when we pledged?"

"I'm ready to 'fess up since you want to know. Thank goodness, I had a sensible Big Sister who didn't want me to stay in a cemetery, either. We went to the movies, went to her parents' house, slept until early in the morning. Then we sneaked back to the cemetery and waited for the rest of the sorority sisters to come." Naomi now had her pocketbook firmly in place over her shoulder. "Make fun of me if you want to, but I'll meet you back at the house." She walked away without acknowledging their calls to her. Her microbraids whipped like a pendulum from her head from her hasty exit.

Naomi's deep-rooted fear offset by her six-foot, athletic frame struck a humorous note in the midst of Athena's grief. She laughed until a loud hiccup cut it off. The laughter helped quell her growing urge to break down into a sobbing heap. But falling apart, and she was on the verge, wouldn't help. No matter what she thought or hoped for, her grandmother was gone.

"I'm ready to go." Athena took a deep breath and exhaled, having made up her mind to deal with the last social aspect of this day.

"Are you sure? Bet your parents won't mind if you didn't want to go back to the house."

Sara's concern touched her. "I'm fine," she reassured her.

Despite her declaration Athena couldn't convince her sorors to let her drive. Sara, always the one to take charge, took the wheel and headed to her parents' house.

They entered her childhood home, where family still lingered. Each room contained relatives in small huddles catching up on each other's lives. Their conversations broke off as Athena moved through each room, accepting their messages of condolences for the third or even fourth time. She almost climbed the stairs out of habit when she remembered that her old bedroom had been given to her visiting aunts.

She interacted for as long as she could stand before slipping away to the in-law suite in the basement where she and Asia stayed. Her sorors signaled that they would join her after they resumed chatting with her parents.

Asia, however, was missing.

Athena figured that a relative nabbed her for a drawn-out discussion on life or on her still-single status.

Thinking about her sister, Athena wondered how she was coping. Just as she had a special relationship with Grandma, Asia also enjoyed a loving, unique one. As twin sisters, they shared many facets of their life with each other. Too many times as twins, they were treated as one with the matching outfits, same after-school activities, and shared birthday celebrations. Grandma's counsel, however, was never offered to them as a set.

She celebrated their individuality like no other, pushing each to forge her own path.

To her surprise, she discovered Asia sitting on the bed, in the room, with a Bible opened in her hands. Athena recognized the gift from Grandma—one for each sister—when they turned twenty-one. Her grandmother felt that a young woman at that age stepping out on her own needed all the fortification she could get.

And God delivered all the help one needed, Grandma always touted.

"I know." Athena could barely get the energy to make her words audible.

Many of the things around the room served as reminders. As her grandmother had grown weaker, she'd come to live with the family. Athena gladly had shared her bedroom, since she soon was leaving for college. She was only too happy to return a smidgen of the kindness shown by her grandmother to her and her other childhood friends.

What she remembered most was that Grandma had been a whiz on the sewing machine and with a crochet needle. Throughout the room, the delicate laced curtains, dainty crocheted doilies on the vanity and quilted bed comforter demonstrated her expert skills.

Asia stepped next to her and slipped an arm around her waist. She rested her head on Athena's shoulder. Most people thought they were identical. But Athena had no problem pointing out the differences between her sister and her.

Unlike Asia, she had a beauty mark on the edge of the left eye. Her right eyebrow had a peak like an upside-down V. On the underside of her arm she had a long scar from climbing over a chain-link fence on her grandparents' farm. The injury required stitches and now a faint scar remained. As far as she was concerned, there were tons more differences, but most people never got that far, completely fascinated that she had a twin.

She stepped away from her sister, trying to keep her body language loose and relaxed.

"Asia." She waited for her sister to catch the change in her voice underlining the serious nature. "I'm leaving my job at the end of the month."

"What? Did you get into an argument with the principal? You're too headstrong, Athena. I've always told you that."

"Thanks for rallying in my corner." Athena smoothed her hair, although it was unruffled. "I'm taking a short break from everything." She reached out to her sister, but she backed away.

"What does that mean?" Asia paused. "What's a short break? You're acting strange and freaking me out."

"Please don't look at me that way." Athena drew a deep breath. She'd been practicing her speech for days. "I don't want this to be a melodramatic moment. Look, you're doing your thing. You've got your job as an account supervisor at that big name health care ad agency. Mom and Dad can't stop yapping about how proud they are of you working on issues like the breast cancer initiative in underserved communities. Who can live up to that? And about two years ago I thought that I was doing my thing. Corporate banking was my path. I got in at the bottom rung with the mortgage and loan department and climbed as far as I could go, hip-deep into middle management. Then I grew tired of working long hours, constantly looking at profit margins, and wondering if my portfolio was big enough to survive the latest employee cuts. One day, Grandma made everything clear to me. She helped me focus on what I want and how to achieve it. And the one thing that is perfectly clear on this dreadful day is that life is too short, especially with our grandmother dying so young—from cancer…in her sixties."

"I don't believe what I'm hearing. When you first suggested this a while ago—leaving your teaching job—I thought you were kidding." Asia's voice shifted from a tone of disbelief to downright anger.

Athena shook her head. "I can't explain what I'm feeling. And why I feel it's urgent. But I need to take this risk to challenge myself and to offer my talents to help others. I want to do something meaningful. I'm twenty-eight years old. It's time."

"Spare me the sanctified BS." Asia's anger bristled from her slender frame. She locked her arms across her chest. "What are you running from?"

Usually she and Asia could finish each other sentences. This time heightened emotions skewed their synchronization. Her sister couldn't or refused to grasp what she tried to say.

No subterfuge was at play. This move wasn't an attention-seeking moment. Athena simply wanted her own identity and the space to fail or succeed. Actually, she needed the space to succeed. Her family modeled the picture-perfect unit of success, in career and family. Failing was not an option. Simply, she didn't know how. And living a life of mediocrity didn't make her feel any better.

Her grandmother had been an innovator in the education field and her parents were equally prominent in academia. Her father was head of the speech pathology department at the Pennsylvania State College. While her mother worked at the Women's Education Frontier, a computer billionaire's nonprofit foundation of top educators studying the role and power of women's education to slowing down global poverty.

Athena wanted to contribute to the family legacy—after other professional detours—with a natural passion for teaching.

But the bureaucracy, standardization of tests and grandiose plans that weren't funded left a bitter taste. Politics had entered her school system and she wasn't having it. Athena wanted out.

"Okay, you'd better start talking," Asia demanded.

"I'm going to be part of a team of teachers."

"And this is different from the teaching job that you're walking away from?"

"I can make a difference in a child's life." Athena pointed to herself.

"Let me get the postcard." Asia rolled her eyes.

"I can keep a child from choosing prostitution or early marriage with education and a chance to step away from a meager future."

"Don't get mad at me. You're the one with the crazy story. You're quitting teaching to go to…teaching." Asia coaxed her along with her fingers. "Continue, I can't wait to hear more."

"I'll be the only U.S. teacher. I'm replacing a sudden vacancy that was advertised in the *International Teacher Corp.*" Athena rushed on, "I'm leaving at the end of the week."

"Whoa, Athena, does Mom know?"

"She knows that I've applied to a couple places…out of town. Well, it's more like out of the country."

"Now you've really lost your mind." Asia stomped her foot, a throwback to the early tantrum years. "How can you do this?"

"What on earth is going on in here?" Sara led the charge, as Naomi and Denise followed up the stairs into the room. "This is not the time to fight."

"We're not fighting." Athena braced herself for the onslaught of questions that would fire at her as soon as Asia blurted her alleged betrayal. "Slightly heated discussion, that's all."

"Athena has lost her mind and is heading out of the country. She's going to some foreign place to find herself and help the natives."

Athena cringed at the thickly laden mockery. "I'm going to teach elementary school kids. What's the big deal? I'll be gone for only six months." She uttered the lie with the quiet hope that Asia accepted the short time frame. Otherwise, news that she would be gone for twelve months to two years would stir another list of questions about her safety and then her sanity.

"Where?" Denise sat on the edge of the bed. She always liked her facts before casting judgment.

"It's a small island called La Isla del Azur, off the southern tip of the Dominican Republic. Literacy levels have plummeted in the past ten years. Meanwhile, prostitution and recruitment into gangs have skyrocketed. The citizens face a really bleak future. Although tourism is the new industry there, the government has to impart the labor force for their skills. They need people from a variety of careers willing to come there and share their skills."

"You don't speak good Spanish, not to get too technical, or any foreign language," Naomi piped in. Her mood had markedly improved now that they were indoors.

"I speak enough Spanish to help them with reading and to teach them English. I recently bought a foreign language tutorial software program. The one that's advertised frequently on TV. Also I've been taking Spanish classes for several months."

"Couldn't you be Joan of Arc here? I'm sure there are some depressed neighborhoods in which you can get all involved." Asia wasn't budging from her disapproving stance.

"Joan led an army. I'm not proposing anything lofty like that. I want to be innovative and inspired. I don't want to deal with my principal's agenda, putting his needs before the children's. Frankly I'm tired of misplaced focus that results in children slipping into the potholes of the system."

"Six months and that's it, right?" Sara, the nurturer of the group, held her gaze.

Athena nodded, wondering if Sara saw into her soul.

Her keen eyes never missed anything. She didn't exhale until Sara nodded and looked away.

"I'm not thrilled about this, but I'll support your need to do this," Sara announced, looking at each soror, long and hard.

Athena had seen Sara use that stoic expression whenever she reviewed a situation, reserving judgment. Each of them had turned to Sara when the stresses of life got to them. She helped—with no conditions attached.

Lying to Sara about the timeline didn't sit well with Athena. Sara had earned loyalty when she helped Denise with her gambling and Naomi with the ugly side of professional basketball. When she could get Sara alone, she'd share all the details. And she'd have to be prepared for Sara's honest assessment of her ability to fulfill this job. Athena wasn't sure that she wanted anyone to deflate her excitement.

"When are you leaving?" Denise stepped into her view.

"Um…next week." Athena clenched her teeth for their protests.

"We barely have time to plan a farewell party," Asia whined, baring her teeth in displeasure over Sara's surrender.

Thank goodness for that. Athena wanted minimal fuss. Her confidence wavered many times. But this was her time to grow without her sister, her family and the heavy-handed presence of her line sisters. This trip served for more than a wish; this was a necessity.

Chapter 2

Collin Winslow waited in the reception area of San Miguel International Airport. Commercial flights at this main airport occurred in the morning and late-afternoon hours. Small private planes, on the other hand, tended to use either of the two smaller airstrips on the island whenever their millionaire owners demanded.

The Stella Maris school project couldn't afford to use private planes for regular business, and not even emergencies. He had used his connections to get an operating budget from the French Teaching Abroad program. They provided the personnel and some money for his idea.

On this morning's flight, he expected two important arrivals. A U.S. publisher had donated several boxes of textbooks. The act had required major groveling on his part, but his tenacity broke through their reservation and red tape. The children would have new math and language arts books, a major accomplishment with the growing number of children attending the school. At thirty years old, his dream had come one step closer to fruition. The students on this island would be given an advantage to attend high school, university or an equally bright industrious future.

He looked up at the tiny TV monitors announcing the latest flights. The airline information he was interested in wasn't posted.

His other reason for this early trip to the airport had equal importance to the mission. The school's foundation, located in the U.S., had selected a teacher, which he had approved. There were teachers from around the world who had also committed to working with his developing nation. In addition, a few local teachers were hired because they really knew what was best for their island's children.

For the U.S. teacher, his excitement measured only halfway on the scale. He'd learned the hard way that most enthusiastic newcomers to his program defected within their first thirty days, heading back to their cushy teaching jobs. But having at least one U.S. teacher was a requirement of the school's board and foundation.

Maybe it was his gut feeling that caused him to bring the large open-bed truck, rather than the school van. The new hire would have to make do without the comfort of a spacious vehicle because he had to haul the boxes of books and luggage. He could see what she was really made of.

Collin glanced up at the TV monitor again, noting the

time displayed in the corner of the screen. The plane was now fifteen minutes late, more than likely held up at the Las Americas International Airport in the Dominican Republic before arriving at its final destination.

Nothing on the island ran according to a set time. His time in the U.S. as a college student at Maryland University and then the beginning of his career as a high school guidance counselor in Prince George's County retrained his expectations of punctuality—the hurry-up mentality. The transition back to the leisurely pace on his homeland La Isla del Azur took some time to get accustomed. Some days he was sure the islanders' laidback attitude would be the death of him. But now, several years later, he now marveled at how work could be done without having to rev the nervous system to hyperspeed.

"Here it comes!"

Collin heard the approaching plane at the same time the person sitting next to him called out. Those eagerly waiting for the plane filled the area in front of the viewing windows. Children, as well as adults, waved and called out for their loved ones.

Collin saved his enthusiasm. After all this trouble to find a new teacher, he hoped she'd last a little longer than the last one. The last teacher from the U.S. had come to the island with a romantic view and unrealistic expectations.

He wouldn't quite label the school compound as simple, but compared to many public and certainly private schools in the States, well, it had several decades to go to catch up with high-tech gadgetry and automatic any and everything. Yet he liked this simple, genuine life and didn't have much patience for these supposed Good Samaritans who couldn't adapt.

Minutes later the stairway was rolled to the open door of the airplane. Collin studied the stream of passengers disembarking. He could spot the tourists among the throng. Pickpockets would, too. The visitors' brightly colored, tropical clothing did nothing to blend them with the locals. The women were a little too put together in their matching short sets, designer shades and stylish purses. The men weren't far behind in their khaki or navy blue shorts, floral Hawaiian-print shirts and wide toothy grins.

Collin stashed his irritation over the arrival of newcomers. After all, the country had only tourism as its basic economy. Tourism meant jobs. But he wanted the next generation to have the option to enter the industry or not.

One passenger trailed the line of people disembarking from the plane. She handled the stairs as if she had never done it before.

Could be the ridiculous heels, he snickered silently.

The inappropriate shoes were one thing, the suit was quite another, making him want to sweat simply looking at her attire. Hair once contained in a ponytail now fought to escape with loose tendrils spilling out in an untidy explosion. He wasn't surprised to see the woman wipe her brow many times before her feet hit the tarmac. She must be here on business to justify wearing such uncomfortable clothing. Otherwise the shirt button-down had to go.

But her innocence and overwhelmed look stirred a little sympathy in him. He couldn't stop looking at her. She's definitely attractive, he supposed. Hopefully she wouldn't trip in those shoes or melt before she got to her destination. It would be a shame to damage those shapely legs.

If he had the time, he'd follow through on the prompting of his body's reaction. But he had no time for mindless flirtation. He studied the legs, again, sliding his view over her hips a few times. Oh, well, time to get to work.

Collin watched the passengers meet their relatives or leave alone in taxis. All, that is, except one. On closer inspection, he realized the lone figure was the woman who didn't understand the true meaning of the words *tropical heat*. She looked like a flower wilting under the humidity, in her navy blue skirt suit and wrinkled white shirt with legs—beautiful legs—encased in black uncomfortable heels.

"Athena Crawford, I presume." He bit down on the inside of his mouth to keep from smiling.

"Yes," she answered in a breathless, harried whisper.

Her severe discomfort might be enough to prove his prediction of desertion back to the U.S. Maybe he should offer to sit with her until that evening when the plane made its return to point of origin.

Too bad, though. Underneath the fatigue and overall moisture, she could be a beauty, but that was even more of a liability. He needed stamina and independence in his teachers, not thick, long hair that had its own mind or facial features that would cause schoolboy crushes.

The public relations firm the school's board had hired pushed him to use his good-looking teachers for brochures and public events. A suggestion that almost brought violence. He had enough of the Hollywood types who had personal agendas seeking media attention while holding a baby from a poor nation in their arms. This project meant more to him than turning into a sellout.

"Are you Mr. Winslow?" Her brown eyes looked at him with so much hope. He was glad to offer her relief with a nod.

"Welcome to La Isla del Azur—The Blue Island." He extended his hand.

"Glad to be here." Her hand gripped his with a confidence that didn't match his perception of her exhausted, weakened state.

"Luggage?"

"I have two pieces and the one that I have here." She glanced down at her feet, where a small suitcase rested on wheels. "I hope that won't be a problem."

"Not at all. I'm picking up several boxes so the large quantity required me to bring a truck. It won't be the most glamorous transport, I'm afraid."

"I'm fine. I appreciate having you meet me because this is all new to me." She ran the back of her hand across her forehead.

"Follow me. I'll take you to the rest of your luggage." Collin led the way through the bustling airport.

The luggage had been brought into a central location. Unfortunately the carousel didn't work, but that was the norm.

"Which one?" He looked over the pile of similarly colored cases. People hovered over the luggage, picking through until they retrieved their own.

"The red ones, over there."

Collin followed the direction to where she pointed.

The two matching upright cases bulged. The bright red sticker with thick, black letters warned that the pieces were heavy.

He signaled one of the porters for assistance. Taking out a twenty, he gladly handed it over with further instructions for retrieving the other cargo.

He pointed toward the exit sign. "We can go to the truck and wait."

They walked through the automatic doors of the airport, leaving the cooler air. The warm tropical morning had settled into place with its heavy-handed presence. Collin glanced over to his new employee to monitor her reaction.

Perspiration dotted the tip of her nose. Equally unsettling was his reaction that sparked to life like a key turned in an ignition of a powerful V-8 engine. Occasionally she licked her lips, a motion that he found disturbingly seductive. His focus rested on the movement and the lingering moisture.

"It will get hotter before midday."

"Oh." She reached into her purse and pulled out a crumpled tissue. Then she played with the top button on her shirt.

Collin knew that would do little to stem her body's cooling. In fact it would take a couple weeks for her body to get used to the humidity and heat. He'd hold the welcome celebration until that time.

"I hate to inconvenience you, but could we stop to get a drink? I'm beyond thirsty." She licked her lips again.

"Of course. If you wait here, I'll get you a soda from the vending machine."

"I'll go with you. That way I can stand in the shade." She hurried toward him, stumbling in the process. Her hand shot out and gripped his arm.

His chin brushed against the top of her head as she lurched toward him. Her hair was soft, like a sheer curtain leaving a light scented trail of freshness. He took a step back but what he really wanted to do was step forward.

"Any particular flavor?" he asked. To his ears, his voice sounded thick. He cleared his throat, blaming it on the dusty surroundings.

"Any soda that is clear, please. I try to stay away from dyes, you know, like colas."

Collin nodded and led the way back into the airport. Pulling out coins from his pants pocket, he slipped the required amount and selected the soda. He handed her the citrus-flavored soda that sported an American brand name.

After a long drink, Athena offered him a big smile.

"Let's get back to the truck. The porters may already be there."

"Oh, dear, I guess we'd better hurry," she said.

This time she led the way until they were outdoors. He waved at the guard as they walked past, toward the parking lot. Because of his work, most people on the island knew him. A perk was being able to park in a restricted area.

"We're here." He stopped next to the truck that looked battered and oversize next to her slight frame. He moved to open the door for her, although it was unlocked.

But she beat his chivalrous action by opening the

door. She hiked up her skirt, stepped up and maneuvered one hip onto the seat. From where he stood, a long, slender leg remained in plain view. The toned muscles worked as she shifted into place.

What the heck was wrong with him?

Ogling women had its time and place—but certainly not while he was at work and not with a member of his own staff.

Until now.

His eyes shifted downward, sweeping from her slender ankle, up past her calf, over her knee, along the muscular definition of her thigh where her skirt obstructed any further viewing.

Her throat clearing snapped his attention. His face warmed with embarrassment. This time he cleared *his* throat and focused on holding the door so that she could adjust herself in the seat. Once he closed the door, he walked around to the driver's side and hopped in.

"I have to head over to the loading area." He repeated what she already knew. But for his sake, he needed to make idle chatter to regain control.

She leaned back her head and wiped her throat.

He wished that she'd stop. Besides actually erasing traces of her moist discomfort, he noted she had a long, graceful neck that suited her overall frame. He hit the brake, a little too sharply, to avoid rear-ending a car ahead of them, jerking both of them in the seats.

"Sorry," he muttered. He scrambled out of the truck and slammed the door shut. His argument with himself continued, as he muttered under his breath. She could be a stunner for all he cared. He didn't need eye candy for the hard work ahead. And if she didn't have the stamina, as he suspected, he'd gladly buy her a one-way ticket.

The next time he had to fill a position, he planned to ask for a photo.

Athena's stomach growled. The soda had quenched her thirst, but now she needed food for the gnawing hunger. The long flight had sapped her energy, leaving her feeling like a half-dead plant, hoping for water after a long drought. Although relieved to arrive safely, she had difficulty soothing her nerves stretched thin from the mixed expectation of her final destination.

On the one hand, a small stirring of excitement ignited her curiosity. However, she didn't like feeling as if she'd abandoned her sister and friends on a lark.

She peered out the truck window to see if he was almost done collecting the luggage. A number of large boxes were being loaded in the back. The vehicle shifted under the weight of its burden.

Sweat prickled her forehead. In desperation, she pulled out her makeup compact to survey the true extent of the damage to her appearance.

She groaned. It was better than crying. She pulled off the ponytail holder and fluffed out her hair. The volume had expanded under the humidity into a soft wavy mass. Around her eyes, the black liner branded to add sophistication and flair now transformed her into a raccoon. The warm beige foundation looked like wet putty on her face, sinking into the natural creases around her mouth and under her eyes.

"What am I doing here?" Athena bit her lip to keep

from tearing up. "This is so not me." She didn't want to be a quitter, but this experience called for a certain type. A type who could handle the thick, sticky humidity. Her scalp prickled from sweat. Her skin turned clammy under the clothing. "What would he do if I asked for my suitcase and headed back into the airport?" She laughed, a sound between pain and frustration.

Thousands of miles separated her from what she knew. Her nerves zinged through her system as if on a caffeine run. She felt her pulse tapping a heightened tempo. All systems would return to normal if she turned and headed back to the plane.

She struggled out of her jacket, pulling the damp blouse from her body. An air-conditioned hotel room would mean the world to her right about now.

The driver's door opened, startling her. Her new boss's face came into view. From the first time she saw him, a frown seemed permanently etched on his forehead. "We're all set."

And in an instant, she opted to maintain her silence. Maybe she wasn't the first to have second thoughts upon arrival, but that didn't mean that she had to give in to leaving, at least not right away.

With a loud roar of the engine, the truck came to life.

Her final destination was the Stella Maris School Project in El Paraiso, Santo Domingo. The foundation that funded the program recruited teachers mainly from the home island and added a teacher from the three main sponsoring countries, including one from the U.S. She had to commit to a year, but also had the option to renew the contract after a performance review. The strong core purpose of the school project pushed for closing the learning gap and providing alternate career choices. Her inner need to be of service intertwined with the mission. She wanted to have success with the students and to make her parents proud. As she took in the scenery and her imagination unfurled with various success stories, she was confident that her grandmother would nod her approval.

She wiped her moist brow, wondering if the humidity would be the unknown variable to make her quit. This Paradise had the temperature of Hades.

"We don't have far to go. The island is only twelve miles long and six miles wide. Lunch will be ready by the time we get there. The school compound houses the teachers. Kids stay off-site with their parents, unless there is an extreme case and then we try to make room for a whole family. But most children have to help around their homes with tasks or other siblings, sometimes contributing to the family income. We get them for only four hours a day, excluding the lunch hour. We try to make those four hours count."

Athena soaked in all the information. She had reviewed the manuals that had been mailed to her in advance, but it didn't take the place of meeting the students and bonding with the other teachers. Already several questions about the compound and the daily duties crowded her thoughts.

As the truck continued to rumble down the narrow roadway, avoiding potholes, other drivers and the occasional livestock, she sensed that in a matter of minutes, she'd have her answers. On that note, she tried to settle back in the seat and enjoy the view. After all, she was in the Caribbean.

"Despite the obvious poverty, this is a beautiful island with proud people."

Athena automatically nodded, startled by her boss's voice: smooth, cultured, deep. She looked out at the landscape, taking in the vivid colors of the land. The people waved at the truck with bright welcoming smiles. At first she didn't respond, but before long, she found herself waving back at the onlookers.

"We're crossing over the dividing line, heading into the Spanish side of the island. It's all one government, but the people have made informal boundaries that contain the groupings of Spanish-, French- and small English-speaking communities. Most of the Caribbean islands shared similar histories with those three empires conquering them at some point."

"And after all that time, people still hang on to those divisions," Athena remarked.

He shrugged. "Some things in life we do without thought because it's easy and predictable."

They turned down a road that was in better condition than the roadway. Athena strained to see through the dense foliage, but either side of the road was like a thick green wall of trees and vines. Unlike the main road they used, this one didn't have any traffic, pedestrian or otherwise.

"There is one driver assigned to the compound. If you need to go anywhere, he'll take you. I'd advise that you take someone into town with you."

"Problems with crime?"

"We have the annoying problems with pickpockets. However, we rarely see deadly violence. Our most common disturbance tends to be fights after drinking too much. Doesn't mean there isn't an element to avoid. But I've warned the staff, and now I'm warning you, not to veer from the law with the wrong crowd or illegal product." He glanced over to her and Athena grew conscious of his examination. "You'll attract attention being new to the island…and your…" He flicked his hand in a quick motion from her head toward her feet.

"Excuse me?"

"Well, they see a woman from the States and immediately they think you'll act a certain way or allow certain behavior. Hollywood has helped to sell that image. Dress conservatively."

"I think that I know how to conduct myself, Mr. Winslow."

"Didn't mean to offend. And we're all informal around here, Athena."

She found his manner prickly and irritating. She had common sense.

Instead of continuing the discussion, he turned on the radio. With calypso music blaring through the truck, they approached a large iron gate.

The concrete fence with barbed wire at its top, the black double gates and isolated location gave only one impression—prison. The Web site photo didn't show the view from her approach. Instead the photo was a closer shot of the school with lots of children intensely participating in class sessions or milling around on the grounds with satisfied grins. That scene drew her here, not this incarcerated style.

"Don't let the level of security scare you. We've got several vans that we use to transport the kids to and from the school and for field trips. We also have computers that were donated and a variety of other expensive school supplies."

Athena nodded.

Two uniformed guards stepped from their guard booths. Holstered weapons were in sight on their hips. They waved at Collin, but scrutinized her.

"This is the new teacher, Athena Crawford. She'll have her new ID on Monday."

"Yes, sir." The taller guard provided a curt nod. "Welcome, miss."

Athena opened her mouth to greet him. The presence of the weapons didn't scare her. Unfortunately schools like her public school in Chicago were no longer safe havens for children. Her gaze shifted and she spied the assault rifles within the guards' reach in the booths. A thick layer of unease rippled down her spine. No doubt these guards meant business. But what level of violence were they so adamantly keeping out? The dryness of her mouth extended to her throat, closing off any sound. Collin revved the engine and rolled through the opened gates.

"You'll notice that the fence doesn't extend to the back side of the property. That's the irony of our high-security facility. There is a wall, but only as a retaining wall for bad weather."

"What about all the movable equipment and furniture, like computers, tables, chairs, copy machines." In Athena's experience, as a teacher in the Chicago public school system, new items tended to take a walk with no chance of recovery.

"We have a tenuous relationship with the organized crime. We don't bother them and in a way, they not only don't bother us, but protect us. One of the former army generals who had delusions of grandeur built this place. He was deposed before he was done. A new owner leases the place to the school. Frankly it was cheaper for us to use a building that didn't need many improvements and large enough for the school and staff dormitories."

Athena smiled, a tad unsettled to hear the colorful history.

Her boss hit the horn twice, blasting away the quiet. Seconds later several doors opened from the buildings surrounding them. Men and women approached the vehicle. Athena followed his actions as he got out of the truck.

"There are only a handful of men who live on the premises. All the women are housed here, including you."

"So much for a hotel room," Athena muttered.

"Our budget doesn't allow for certain amenities."

Athena bit her lip, a bit embarrassed at being caught complaining.

I knew what I was getting into when I applied.

"Cicely, Thelma and Lorraine, this is Athena. Make sure you show her the ropes. I'll complete the orientation around the facilities tomorrow. I'm sure that she'd like to freshen up before lunch."

The three women closed their huddle around her, shepherding her toward the farthest bungalow-styled building.

She hadn't been introduced to the men. But when she looked over her shoulder, Collin had their attention with instructions about unloading the truck. One of the younger guys had the job of following the women with her luggage.

Not for the first time today, Athena wondered what she'd gotten herself into.

New job.

New home.

New boss…who could give a young version of Poitier a run for his money.

Chapter 3

Athena looked toward the open door and then again at Collin, waiting for a reassuring sign from him that she'd be okay. Not that she didn't trust the women hovering to meet her, but so far the only person she'd bonded with was him.

"Hi, Athena, welcome."

Athena turned toward the enthusiastic greeter who stepped forward. The young woman's sunny disposition and American accent reassured her.

"I'm Cicely. Come on in."

"Where are you from?" Athena was glad that there was some type of connection with a coworker.

"I'm from L.A. Wasn't such a stretch to come here—weather-wise. People are a heck of a lot nicer, let me tell you."

Athena nodded, not sure what else to do. Cicely had a mega serving of energy that she hoped wasn't a morning trait.

"Let's get you to your room. I'm Thelma." Another smiling woman approached her. While Cicely had the blond girl image working in her favor, Thelma was a quiet brunette, with a strong accent. When she saw the curiosity in Athena's expression, she added, "I'm an Aussie."

Thank goodness she didn't make the mistake of asking if she was British. While Cicely could turn a few heads with her fresh, girly-girl disposition, Thelma reminded her of Jaclyn Smith—wholesome and elegant. Hopefully she could fit in. She had to fit in.

While Cicely and Thelma argued about who would show her to her room, Athena looked out through the door. Not only was the doorway her exit from this new place called home, but it framed Collin like a life-size portrait of male physical prowess. Maybe he knew that he was being watched.

Her gaze had its own zoom focus, honing in on him unbuttoning his shirt and slipping it off well-defined shoulders. He tossed the shirt onto the side of the truck. And as if he wanted the world to see, he placed his hands on his hips and stretched back. She saw arms, forearms and flat stomach with the dark smoothness of his complexion glistening under the sun's heat. Lean, sinewy muscles flexed, adding a touch of excitement to her secret delight. How in the world was she going to keep a level head around this man? Her body already reacted whenever he was near and now he'd managed to turn up the dial on her internal thermometer hovering just below the simmer line.

He was a man in charge, with arrogance and control issues in abundance. Traits she found annoyingly sexy.

Her married and unmarried line sisters would've gone juvenile, enjoying this exhibition. No doubt she'd probably have to beat back Naomi and her sister, Asia, from choosing straws to select the lucky one to go talk to him. Sara and Denise would've moaned at the fact that they were off the market.

Now Asia had enough spunk to step up to the challenge, but she wasn't into pursuing any man. Naomi, on the other hand, went after her men the way she played basketball for a pro women's team—aggressive and ultimately successful.

Pursuing a man sounded desperate. She sneaked in another glance at Collin. Acting on opportunities was simply innovative and entrepreneurial.

"Um…Athena? Did you have more luggage?"

"Excuse me?" Athena pulled her gaze from Collin's physique to her new coworker, Cicely. "Oh, yes…er, no. This is it."

Cicely had the two suitcases and carry-on tucked under her arm.

"Please, I'll take those." Athena reached for the bags.

Her silly behavior had displayed bad manners. She was more than embarrassed.

"Not a problem." Cicely led her down the hall past a series of rooms on either side.

The front area had been decorated like a sitting room with three conversation areas. The kitchen and dining area were on the opposite side from the rooms forming the other horizontal portion of the T-shaped building.

"We have rooms for eight teachers. Right now, with you here, we total four females and three males in the other building. There are four bathrooms. Every two bedrooms share a bathroom. Here's your room. I hope you don't mind being at the end. The room attached to your bathroom is empty. Figured you'd like your privacy."

Cicely unlocked the door and stepped aside.

"Wow, are you sure this is for me?" Athena slowly entered her new sleeping area.

The room resembled a hotel suite in a brochure for an island vacation. Blue and white floral-printed bedcoverings set against the light-colored furniture and wicker pieces suited the tropical backdrop. *So lovely,* she thought.

Cicely laughed. "Actually all the rooms are decorated in similar style. But the end rooms have a tad more space. And of course, more windows, which, for you, looks out into the vegetable garden. The classrooms get the ocean view, not always the best choice when you're trying to hold the children's attention."

"It's beautiful." Athena meant it.

"I'll let you get settled. Would you like some lemonade? I'm sure you're parched."

Athena's stomach growled. "Sorry."

"Lunch will be ready in a few minutes. We tend to eat our main meals during the middle of the day. In the evening, we have supper which is a lighter fare."

"I'm looking forward to all of it." Athena, with a rueful grin, patted her tummy.

Cicely closed her door, her retreating footsteps beating a steady rhythm against the wooden floors.

Athena remained in place until the footsteps faded

and the trilling calls of the birds outside seeped into her consciousness. Now she had no regrets. Didn't mean that a few doubts didn't rear its head, but she'd done it. With minimal pomp and circumstance, she'd stepped onto the path of her grandmother's journey.

After exploring the bathroom and opening the wardrobe in her room, she moved to the louvered window. The unique window, a natural element in the Caribbean setting, opened as she unwound the lever. Each pane of glass moved from a downward slant to a flat plane, opening the view to the lush vista.

In more ways than she could ever imagine, she had pushed open the curtain to her life.

Only an hour ago she had entertained the possibility of returning home. But there were too many opportunities for her passion and growth to cave into her insecurities. She didn't believe it was insecurity, though, when she sensed that Collin watched her with some sort of expectation. She'd say something and the corner of his mouth twitched. She'd react to their conversation and his reply grew curt.

Maybe he was disappointed in the foundation's selection. She had something to prove. If her beating a hasty retreat back to the U.S. was his goal, he'd have to wait a while for her surrender.

A soft knock at her door snapped close the meandering path to homesickness. She ran her hands over her face to wipe away signs of sadness and to cover her emotions with a bright, ready smile. "Come in."

Cicely popped her head into the room. "Lunch is ready."

"Great. I'm famished."

They entered the dining area, which had a large wood table that could feed a small party at a banquet. The other teachers were seated, but a few more empty spots remained, although set with plates and silverware.

"Cicely, where are the men?" Thelma asked. Her irritation marked not only in her dour tone, but also the frown set in place.

"They came to the table on time, but looking as if they'd played in the dirt. I sent them to get cleaned up."

Athena looked up at the sound of Lorraine's voice. Her solid frame and her thick gold braids on either side of her head added to the look of a Valkyrie. A French accent, however, skewed the Nordic goddess resemblance.

Thelma bumped her elbow. "She's our enforcer."

"I can believe that," Athena replied.

"I'm not waiting all day," Cicely complained. "Let's say grace."

Just then, the front door swung open with a loud burst from three men, talking and laughing. From where she sat, Athena smelled the soap that must have had active use. Each vigorously wiped his feet on the bristles of the welcome mat.

Lorraine's approving grunt was a sign for them to continue over to the table. Athena was amazed that these muscular men who oozed testosterone were like schoolboys under Lorraine's critical gaze.

"Well, stop gawking and introduce yourselves," she ordered. Her role of den mother rang clear.

"I'm Gus. I teach French and math."

"Hi. I'm Marcus. I teach Spanish and English and writing."

"Bill. I teach science."

"Hi, guys, I'm Athena. I'm teaching reading and language arts." They all seemed friendly enough and she was grateful not to have to undergo some type of initiation to the group, although it was only the first day. If anyone would put her through the ringer, it might be the women, specifically Lorraine.

Their chairs scraped against the floor, eliciting a hiss from Lorraine and a series of apologies. The hub of activity didn't pull Athena's attention from one fact: Collin wasn't there.

"What about Mr. Winslow? Does he eat with his staff?" Athena piped up before Thelma began grace.

"Everyone calls him Collin. He doesn't eat with us, especially on the weekend. He lives off-site."

"Oh." Athena didn't have time to think about that revelation before she had to bow her head as Thelma said the blessing.

"Let's eat!" Cicely declared.

Athena took the dish of corn on the cob that was offered to her. In a short time, she had almost covered the open space on her plate with a variety of colorful vegetables and portion of roasted chicken.

"Hey, just because we've got a new person in the ranks doesn't mean that we have to be shy. We're never this quiet. Stop pretending as if we're in church." Lorraine spooned another helping of stewed tomatoes.

"Collin said you'd be starting right away. Are you sure you want to start that quickly?" Bill asked.

"She's capable," a familiar, deep voice drawled.

Athena's fork clattered against her plate. Collin stood in the doorway, his penetrating gaze latched on to her face. She noted that he'd also cleaned up wearing fresh clothing.

Each person around the table offered an enthusiastic greeting. Athena offered a short wave because if she gave in to the quickening of her pulse, a nervous giggle would erupt.

The man exuded a strange pull on her senses.

"Slide over, Bill." Collin took the seat next to Athena. "My housekeeper fixed one of *her* favorite dishes that's not one of mine." He helped himself to the various dishes that were now more than half-empty. "Do you like your room?"

Athena nodded, hastily swallowing her food. "I'm so pleased by how nice and welcoming it is. It's comparable to a hotel."

"We want the staff to be as comfortable as possible because this is home for the year."

The conversation over lunch stayed in the general interest category, safe and not intrusive. Everyone fired questions at her, poking through her background and her journey to their mutual workplace. Everyone, that is, but Collin. He chatted about various topics, but never asked her questions about herself. However, she took the opportunity to listen for any clues that revealed her boss's character.

"Hey, looks like you're fading fast," Lorraine declared. She flipped back one of her braids with one hand, while holding the fork like a spear.

Athena tried to subdue a yawn. "I'm sorry. Guess the

travel and heat are catching up with me. I promise to be more energized once I've recuperated."

Lorraine waved away her apologies. "After lunch, go catch a nap. This evening we're heading in town for the drive-in movies."

"Drive-in?" Athena had never in her life gone to a drive-in movie. Her generation preferred stadium seating, surround-sound movie theaters. Only couples who wanted to get their freak on went to drive-in movie theaters. She glanced around the table at the diverse cast of characters. Nope. They didn't strike her as the freaky types.

At that moment, Collin turned to her. *Why does it always feel like he's assessing or studying me?* She didn't want to think about whether he would get busy in the backseat of a car. But she couldn't help herself. What was his type? Was he a butt and boobs guy? Was he into trophy girlfriends? Did he secretly crave to be a boy toy for an older, rich woman?

Her cheeks warmed at the possibilities.

Windows foggy. Car rocking. Tight confinement. And those dark brooding eyes hovering *over* her. She sputtered. Eyes not over her, but over…a woman.

"Here, seems like you need a drink." He pushed his untouched glass toward her.

Athena gulped the water, praying that the only overt physical reaction was her cough. What he spiked elsewhere made her want to squirm like a kid at an all-day session at church.

"You've never been to a drive-in movie?" Bill asked.

Athena shook her head.

"We can take the school van. Sometimes we go in the picnic area off to the side to enjoy the movie while eating dinner," Bill explained. His Trinidadian accent flowed over every word.

"Sounds like fun." She hoped that she sounded enthusiastic and like a team player. Her preference for consuming food was at a table. But she had embarked on an unexpected journey, so why would anything else be normal?

"Collin, are you going to the reception at the British Embassy tonight?" Cicely asked with a strange eagerness.

"Yes. While you all are having fun at the movies, I'll be working on getting contacts for more donations. Someone has to do the boring parties."

"I envy you." Cicely smiled, her face taking on a dreamy expression.

Athena guessed that Cicely was the youngest, or had been, until her own arrival. The young woman thrived on displaying her over-the-top emotions. She wondered if Cicely's desire extended beyond simply attending the reception. Did she want that invitation to be personally extended by Collin?

"Cicely, I do have an extra ticket. Would you like to come?"

"Oh, could I? Thank you, Collin. You're the best."

Athena tried to quell the envious stab. Attending an embassy function was a big deal. Who wouldn't want that experience? Now she had to listen to Cicely's excited chatter about what she'd wear.

The men excused themselves from the table. Lorraine's eyes critically watched over their progress with clearing the dishes. Collin also did his share of the labor and then stepped away from the group.

"Dinner was great, as always, Lorraine." Collin touched his forehead in a salute. "Tell Cicely to be ready at seven o'clock sharp. I'm not waiting."

Lorraine nodded. "I'll tell her six-thirty. That way, she should be ready."

They all shared a laugh.

Athena remained where she was, hovering between the dining area and the kitchen. She noted that Collin left without any special remark to her. Even "Have a good night" would have been appreciated. Maybe he wasn't one for sentimentality. On the other hand, *she* liked the little niceties of life. There would be time to break him into her quirks.

With three strong females, she'd have to assert her style in here.

"Athena, you'd better get your rest for the movies tonight," Thelma advised.

"I need help for this evening."

"Oh, Cicely, stop carrying on like a girl on her first date," Lorraine scolded, still cleaning up in the kitchen.

Thelma waved off Lorraine's remarks. "Don't worry, I'll help you. Now let's send you in something that will knock off a few socks. If you know what I mean."

Thelma winked at Athena and disappeared into Cicely's room. Lots of giggling ensued.

Athena closed her bedroom door. For a brief moment, she had a flashback to university life and her sorors after they'd pledged. Frankly she was a little taken aback by Cicely's open infatuation with Collin.

Even worse than that, he did nothing to squelch the behavior. His manner was casual, assured, maybe even expectant toward his employee's bias.

Yes, he had all the attributes to make a young girl weak at the knees. As the new woman on the scene, he might have the same expectation for Athena. After all, he had been checking out her body with brazen openness.

She climbed into the bed. Her thoughts drifted drowsily through the gallery of new faces. She closed her eyes, drifting to sleep with the image of Collin Winslow shirtless and smiling.

"Athena?" A soft knock sounded.

Athena opened her eyes, furiously fighting the heaviness of her sleepy state. The room had darkened, bringing on her confusion. For a few seconds she wondered where she was.

A familiar voice called to her. Athena rubbed her eyes and stretched.

"Lorraine, please come in."

"I tried waking you up earlier, but you were knocked out. We're getting ready to leave."

"Do you mind if I miss it this time? I'm sorry that I won't make it, but I'm a little out of it." Athena yawned.

"I understand. I just didn't want you to wake up and be alarmed when you realized we were all gone. Tomorrow you'll feel much better, I promise." Lorraine stepped out and closed the door.

Quiet descended onto the house once the others had left for the drive-in. She must have missed Cicely's departure, too.

She wandered into the kitchen barefoot and in her

lounging pants and T-shirt. She'd unfettered herself from the bra. Like clockwork, her stomach rumbled. A hammock on the back deck invited her. However, she was a little skittish with going outdoors not knowing what species of nightlife existed.

She peered out of the window, looking up at the sky. Somehow she expected the night to be inky black. Instead the sky was several shades lighter than midnight blue. Stars sparkled and the moon cast its glow, cutting a path across the vast property.

Before settling on the couch and turning on the TV, she went to turn on each light switch, including the fan. Instead of choosing a thriller, she chose a British romantic comedy to keep her company. When all else failed, a good romance book or movie was a necessary tool in life's survival kit.

Collin didn't really mind the extra task associated with his job to network and hobnob with deep pockets. He loved his school and its potential to risk complaining too much about an embassy reception.

What he didn't like was the attention received because of his single status. The more he resisted, the more tenacious became his followers. He was glad that Cicely accompanied him. She made him laugh with her infectious personality. But she also served to keep the more aggressive types at bay.

"Looks like they are busting at the seams." Cicely turned her body sideways to enter after the security check.

"We're probably breaking all kinds of fire laws," Collin acknowledged.

Only in Paradise

These embassy parties were proving to be popular, especially among the younger jet-setters. A lifestyle that was completely foreign to him.

"Okay, I've got my eyes fastened on Target A." Cicely primped her hair and smiled at him. She whipped her head and threw back her shoulders.

"Go get your next victim."

"You're not funny, but I do follow orders well." Cicely adjusted her dress and strutted toward the newest arrival to the British diplomatic corp. Fresh-faced and looking like he'd just left his mother's care, the young man succumbed easily to Cicely's sexy aura. The young woman certainly knew how to weave her web. She didn't have to say a word. Her hips did all the talking.

Collin chuckled and resumed focus on his purpose. He headed over to the British ambassador, who had become an advocate of the school program after two years of pressing him to take a look at the accomplishments.

"Wesley, good to see you." Collin shook the ambassador's hand. "I see your staff talked you into throwing another party."

"I choose to call it a reception," the ambassador replied. "I can't believe that I have a rock band."

"It's a sign of the times and now you're the best party on the block."

"What a reputation to earn." The ambassador grew serious and took his elbow. "Let's get to a quiet spot. I want to hear how things are going for you."

Collin gladly followed the ambassador. They entered a series of rooms, going through connecting doors, to the ambassador's office.

Doors, instead of windows, surrounded the room. Sparsely furnished in dark leather and highly polished wood, the room modeled efficiency instead of high-design. But such trivial things didn't matter to Collin.

The ambassador offered a cigar, which Collin waved off. His bouts with childhood asthma took care of any temptation to smoke. Sitting in a closed room with a strong-smelling cigar didn't bode well, either.

"I don't really smoke these unless I have to. I got them as a gift. I noticed that some people need to smoke a cigar to make a deal or agree on a deal." The ambassador sniffed the length of the cigar.

"My lungs dictate my choices."

"My heart probably does the same if I actually listened to it." Wesley patted his stomach and grinned. "The wife would love to get me into the doctor's office, but you know how that goes. I'm not ready to return home."

"Do you think that you'd have to?" Collin wondered if Wesley knew more about his health than he let on.

His wife tended to stay in England during the summer months and headed to La Isla del Azur in the winter months. Collin had his private thoughts about such an arrangement. But his reservations didn't match the success of their voluntary separation.

"I'm now getting up there in age. Going bald, getting fat, people around me are young enough to be my grandchildren. Soon I'll be put into the pastures."

"You've never sounded so…mature. Where is all this coming from?"

Wesley waved his hand. A tired chuckle shook his

frame. "Maybe it's these receptions that make me feel old. Don't follow my lead and wait all your life to do things for humanity."

"That's dramatic. You've been in the international arena for decades. And what you've done for the children on the island has been phenomenal."

"You've helped with a lot of the work."

"Well, I need your help once more."

Ambassador Piedmont leaned forward. His eyes lit up with interest. He beckoned with his hand. "Come on, I want to hear your latest bright idea."

"For the first time, we'll have a handful of students at the high school level. I want a scholarship program to be created for graduates to go to England for university."

"I'm thinking that there's more."

"I want some of your rich buddies to pick up the tab." Collin paused for his benefactor's response.

"That sounds reasonable enough, but—"

"But I may face stiff opposition." Collin hated the bureaucracy tied to getting much-needed funds.

"To say the least. Your prime minister will most likely object that his citizens shouldn't be sent to a colonial power to be brainwashed. My government's conservative constituents will argue that we don't have space to educate in our universities."

"For approximately ten children. Give me a break!" Collin pursed his mouth. "My apologies."

"I'm only sharing the reality."

"But will you help me? We're making progress. Kids are coming off the streets. Parents have hope. And the pimps and prostitute industry won't get a chance to recruit." Collin refused to let Wesley's caution dampen his zeal. His school had a great staff of teachers. He had a good international program underwriting his school. He was on the edge of gaining momentum.

"I'll do what I can. I do have to fly back to England at the end of the week. I'll start talking to my colleagues."

Collin grinned. "Thank you. I can't ask for much more."

"But you will, won't you? Now let's go party."

"I'm afraid that I'm going to have to get going." Collin had the meeting that he needed to have. He hadn't expected to be able to get the ambassador to himself. But the opportunity was perfect timing.

He could head for the drive-in and hang out with the others. But he was too wound up and they wouldn't appreciate his talking shop while they tried to relax and watch the movie. They'd scolded him on that many times.

Yet he wasn't in the mood to work. Maybe he'd head back to the school and go through the stack of papers that needed his attention. Now to find Cicely.

After circling the reception, he finally spotted her. "Cicely, I'm ditching the party."

"Cool, I think I've got a ride home."

"Nope. I'm sending the driver to get you."

"And what if I have other plans?"

Collin sighed. "You only just met. Could be a nutcase for all you know."

"You really know how to kill a mood. Haven't you heard of chemistry? Sometimes you just know and you go with it."

"Like I said, the driver will be waiting for you." Cicely was the all-American girl—smart, beautiful, sexy…and stubborn. Thank goodness she was a good teacher. But her libido seemed to be in overdrive. However, as long as her extracurricular activities didn't interfere with her work, he would step aside.

Back at the school compound, Collin called the driver and instructed him on his assignment for the night. He headed to the office, welcoming the solitude. As he strode across the property, he glanced over to the women's house.

A shadow crossed the window. He paused. No one should be home. And he surely didn't beat Cicely back to the house. Forgetting his office for the moment, he walked to the house. As he hit the first step, the front door opened.

Athena screamed.

What felt like a missile sailed through the air and hit him squarely in the forehead. When he sank down to his knees, he heard Athena babbling. The cool, sweet taste of vanilla ice cream rolled down his face past his mouth.

His last conscious thought was of Athena two inches from his face talking to him, but he couldn't focus. Her mouth repeated his name. He couldn't hear.

Nice lips. If he only had the energy to pucker.

He blinked, sinking into darkness.

Chapter 4

"Mr. Winslow?" Athena tapped the side of her boss's face. She hadn't meant to give him a lobotomy with the bowl of ice cream, but he'd scared the mess out of her. "Mr. Winslow, please open your eyes…Collin?"

"I think my brain is sitting in the front yard."

Athena was too worried to figure out if he was being funny or sarcastic. She allowed him to lean on her while he struggled into a seated position. According to her first-aid lessons, victims of head injuries shouldn't be moved. However, she couldn't stop him. She inhaled, holding her breath in horror as she watched Collin get on all fours, reaching out for the doorknob instead of her to steady his progress to his feet.

"Ice cream is everywhere. You'd better clean that up before the bugs come. I'm going to make my way to the couch and die for a quick second," he said through gritted teeth.

Athena hesitated, moving toward him to assist in his labored walk to the couch before he waved her off. Keeping an eye on him, she headed to the kitchen to get the necessary cleansers. She certainly didn't want any unwelcomed visitors of the creepy-crawly variety in the house. Quickly she cleaned the area of its residual stickiness. She looked down at herself and realized that her T-shirt revealed too much. She ran to her room and put on a robe before heading back.

From where she kneeled on the floor, Athena was inches from Collin's face. Close enough to see the tension, although his eyes were closed. His mouth drew tight, as if fighting back the pain. If only she'd waited a few seconds at the door for his figure to emerge into the light. Then she'd be sharing her ice cream rather than wiping it off the floor.

A small bump formed over his right eye. Physical evidence of her action staring back at her. She wrung her hands. What to do now?

She continued to stare down at his face. Although minor damage had occurred, the imperfection didn't mar the handsome face.

His smooth skin tone showed off a rich, dark coffee boldness. From the sharp outline of his lips that were perfectly full and a hard masculine contour, to his prominent, blunt nose, and… Her thoughts snapped into smithereens.

He opened his eyes and locked onto her in a hypnotic gaze, drawing her into its inky depth. She moved closer to him, creeping forward until the couch stopped her progress.

His hand reached toward her. Her breath hitched. Once his fingers touched her cheek and cupped the side of her face, she exhaled. Gently he guided her face to his. Athena complied; her pulse quickened with anticipation. She could almost taste his kiss.

His gaze shifted to her lips. On cue they responded, opening slightly as they touched his, molding along the lines of his mouth. She closed her eyes to savor the moment, for how long could this last? Her hands, thankfully, didn't wait for permission to slide under his body, as his arms encircled hers. Her breasts crushed against his chest.

Time meant nothing. Her lips sparked to life under the ministrations of his tongue that coaxed and teased her nerve endings. Every part of her from the roots of her hair to the tips of her toes reacted to the new sensation of being awakened. He worked her mouth like a craftsman with his expert tool, flicking her inhibitions away.

Her robe slid off one shoulder and she shrugged her other shoulder to finish the job. His hand slid under the thin, semi-sheer T-shirt and touched her lower back. Like a juggernaut, his fingers transmitted a shock wave of heat throughout her system.

She craved his touch and ached for his hand to slide over her hip. The small movement of his hand along the side of her body teased her nipples into tightening. This man was methodically waking up each part of her body into a sensual swoon. Below her belly button, her body blushed in full response.

Athena pulled away and arched back, gasping for air. Her entire body was on fire. She felt throbbing between her legs. Her breasts rose and fell with exertion. She slowly opened her eyes to the bright lighting of the room, and to his eyes looking back at her. Their expression no longer held the intensity that ignited their passion.

"Sorry." He pulled his hands from her body and pushed himself to sitting position. "I…well, I don't know…" He touched the bump, shaking his head while the frown deepened.

Athena pulled her robe closed and turned away. Her face now burned from embarrassment. How had this happened? She wiped at her face, trying to smooth her hair in the process. Reality forced its entrance, shining a harsh light on her actions and reactions.

She heard him move. A few deep, painful grunts escaped. The couch squeaked its protest. Then his feet appeared near her. The moment to be judged had come. How would she plead if she had to go to trial?

Athena rose, knowing that what had just occurred was definitely in the past. There would be no future repeat.

"I shouldn't have done that." Collin stared into her eyes; gone was the dreaminess that maybe she only imagined. "What I did was *inexcusable*." He stepped away from her. His face set in a grim mask. "I hope my actions don't make your choice to be here distasteful."

"I'm fine." Telling her new boss that she liked the kiss was out of the question. Maybe later tonight when the excitement had gone out of her body and common sense was allowed back in, she'd provide a free pass for remorse.

Instead her back was a little straighter. Her chin rose a tad higher. She dared him to look at her.

The sound of a car driving up, with a sweep of headlights across the living room, broke the tension. Muffled voices grew louder until Athena recognized Lorraine's distinctive voice telling everyone to keep it down.

She surveyed her appearance in the mirror, tightening the belt around her robe to the point where it was uncomfortable. She glanced over to Collin to see if he was alarmed. He hadn't said a word since his declaration. He headed for the door. They needed closure. But she sensed that wasn't going to happen.

The front door opened and Lorraine and Thelma burst into the room, but stopped short. "Oh," they remarked in unison.

Lorraine took the lead. Her scrutiny covered Athena, then Collin, who now stood near the doorway. He still didn't face her. His shoulders were stiff.

"I stopped by to see if Cicely had come home." Finally he turned around. "Please let me know when she returns. Lorraine, because Athena starts on Monday, show her around tomorrow. She'll shadow you with the young teenagers until I determine otherwise."

"I'm sure she'll do fine." Lorraine smiled, but it faded when he didn't respond. Instead she looked over to Athena, pinning her with her intense blue eyes. The cool assessment surprised Athena, leaving her a bit unsettled.

"I'm looking forward to starting. Teaching is what I want to do." Athena paused. "It's why I'm here." She meant every word. Despite what had happened only minutes ago, and what Collin might think, she had a mission. "I can't wait to get started."

"We'll see." Collin finally looked at her. She expected to see acknowledgment for what had transpired between them, but his masked expression shielded any reaction he may have had.

Athena bit down the disappointment. Not that she wanted to engage in a fling with her boss. Or did she? She pulled her arms around her body and turned away. "Think I'll turn in for the night."

The front door closed. Athena didn't have to turn around to feel Lorraine's stare on her back. This was worse than having a resident attendant in charge of her freshman dorm. She continued her retreat to her room. For the first time that day, she wished Asia was sharing her room like they did as teens, when she could bare her soul and get sisterly advice.

But she'd chosen this path and she refused to give in to the fear of failing. Instead, she used the time to write her experiences about day one in Paradise.

Collin spent a restless night thinking about the egregious error he'd committed. What madness had entered his mind to kiss Athena? She was an employee. He was the boss. She'd done nothing but look at him. No wink had summoned him. No batting of the eyelashes had called him. Maybe it was when she had surveyed his face, thinking that he was unaware. He'd seen the slight movement of her mouth and felt compelled to cover it with his lips. Nothing made sense.

As the sun began its ascent above the mountain, he

gave up on trying to sleep. Instead he pulled on a pair of shorts, socks and running shoes. For the next hour, he jogged along the beach, waving to the few early risers. Even the morning proved to be humid. His body could handle the conditions before the midday sun turned the place into a scorcher.

He pushed himself, running faster, harder. His arms pumped beside him, propelling him forward. He willed his muscles to work to the point of exhaustion. Anything to banish the nagging memory of the kiss. Even now, his body reacted and Collin ramped up his speed. Maybe she wouldn't work out at the school and be out of his life before he made a complete fool of himself.

A person didn't get far in life underestimating the people around him. Yet Collin knew he'd done that with Athena.

He'd dismissed her as spoiled and self-absorbed. But her quirks masked the spirit that sought solutions in places that weren't popular. And the reason he'd approved of the selection came down to intelligence and success in her previous jobs. Simply, she was a go-getter.

A woman with more body than mind was a waste of time. One with more mind than body intrigued him. But when all the planets aligned, that didn't open the door to do stupid things like surrender to a kiss.

First he'd expected her desertion. Now he wanted it for his sake.

Breakfast, after his run, consisted of a light fare of tropical fruit that he ate on his veranda. He looked out over the property behind his home, a former sugar cane plantation. Now he farmed several acres of vegetables and fruits which not only fed the children as part of the lunch program, but he also sold the rest to the town markets and a wholesaler who supplied various embassies and other diplomats for their parties.

"Will you be working at home, Mr. Winslow?"

Collin swung around when his housekeeper spoke from the doorway. "Not sure. Does it matter?"

"No, Mr. Winslow. I didn't know whether you would require lunch?"

He shook his head. "Don't worry about lunch, Lynette. And I'll be working the barbecue grill this evening for dinner. Weren't you supposed to be off? Go put up your feet."

"Thank you, Mr. Winslow."

His housekeeper turned and left. Collin resumed looking out at the verdant landscape. He had deliberately sought a home away from the school to give himself his own space. So far it had worked, helping him to prevent burnout from the tedious side to his life's work.

But he did have work to do in the office. And for all he knew, Lorraine may need him to help with Athena's orientation. But he wouldn't think of intruding. He'd let them know he was there and if Lorraine needed assistance, he was on hand.

Juice from a slice of papaya he ate spilled on his shirt. The smear didn't go away despite rubbing it vigorously with a napkin. He'd have to change. Several minutes later, he was still flicking through the rack of clothing. The staff always came for Sunday dinner at his house. He didn't want to select a shirt that was too busi-nesslike. But he didn't want to look as if he was a carefree student without ten cents in his pocket, either. He rubbed his jaw. He needed a shave right after he made his selection.

Two shirts had potential. He stood in front of the mirror whisking one in front of him and then the other. Not that he really cared, but the cranberry did look better on him. And the host should look his best. He flexed his biceps and abs, pleased with the view. Not that there was anyone to care.

"Sir."

"Lynette, you could knock." He whisked both shirts behind his back. He shifted from one leg to the other, wishing that the hot flush would subside from his face. Plus, Lynette had the look of a grandmother type and the intuitive skills to go along with the image.

"I did knock, but because the door was open—"

"Never mind. It's okay." He waited for her to continue.

"Lorraine is on the line. She sounds a bit upset."

"What happened?"

"She didn't say. But she said that it was urgent that she speak with you." Lynette looked at him, clearly hesitating over her next bit of news. "She was crying."

Collin thanked her, waving her out of the room. He waited until she closed the door before hurrying to the telephone at his bedside. "Lorraine, what is it?"

"Sorry to bother you so early."

"I'm already up. Did something happen to Athena?" He didn't want to go down that path to think about what could've happened to her.

"Ah, no." Her surprise came through quite clearly. The question in her tone hovered through the telephone. "It's Cicely."

"Didn't I tell you to call me when she got in?"

"I couldn't. She only returned home this morning, looking a little worn-out."

Collin sighed with relief. "Okay, and how is this different from any other time?"

"She's been attacked."

"What?" Collin threw the shirts on the bed and grabbed a T-shirt. "No one around here would dare touch you ladies." He didn't share how he knew this.

"It happened."

"I'm sending Dr. Singh over to see her right now." Collin hung up. His thoughts raced through the probability of events that led up to this moment. His face hardened into a grim mask.

"Lynette, call Dr. Singh. There's been a situation over at the teachers' compound. I'm heading over there."

"Yes, Mr. Winslow. Let me know if you need anything done here. I'll be here."

Collin nodded. He dressed, this time without thinking about how he looked. One of the main points of his employment was a safe environment. He had the promise of the government and extracted a guarantee from the less desirable elements that his staff would be protected.

His erratic driving caused a few near-misses, but he finally pulled into compound. For the early hour, the placed buzzed with nervous energy. Even the guard on duty changed his demeanor as if protecting a military fort. The men stood out on the porch in a tight huddle, smoking and chatting. Thelma ran out to meet his car, her eyes reflecting her worry.

"Dr. Singh is with her." Thelma pointed back at the door.

"How bad is it?" he asked. He hurried up to the partly opened door. He entered, scanning the living room. Athena stood in the hallway, looking at the door of Cicely's room. She glanced over at him, but returned to her duty of monitoring the door.

Just then Lorraine emerged from the room with the doctor. No one said anything until he approached them.

"I'll go make some coffee," Lorraine offered and headed for the kitchen. "Athena, come help me. Thelma, ask the men if they want coffee."

Collin silently thanked Lorraine for getting everyone busy with tasks so that he could confer with the doctor. He walked over to a quiet corner of the room, guiding the doctor by the elbow to join him.

"How is she doing? Was she…?" Collin couldn't bring himself to say the words.

"She's resting. Of course, she's shaken up, poor girl. She wasn't raped."

Collin exhaled. "Does she need to be in a hospital?"

Dr. Singh shook his head. "I would have sent her myself if I thought she was in any danger."

"Who would do this?" Collin burst out.

"Her attacker wasn't a man."

"What?" Collin stared at the doctor's turban as if a revelation would occur.

"She was attacked over a man. She has scratches

on her cheek. And a bruised rib where she was kicked."

"What on earth? I've got to call the police."

"Ah, Mr. Winslow, I think you should talk to her before doing that. Her pride is in shambles. She might not take kindly to your gesture." The doctor's bushy eyebrows wiggled at him with its underlying message.

He got it. But he didn't agree. Nevertheless, he would talk to Cicely and convince her that she had to follow through with the law.

"I gave her a mild painkiller. She'll rest and be healed in no time. But her emotional state could be rocky."

Collin grunted. The doctor knew a thing or two about the physical body, but he may underestimate Cicely's healing ability of the mind. She was a fighter. From her first day on the job, she'd worked hard to convince everyone that she was mature enough to handle the job and its rigors.

"Coffee is ready."

Collin looked up at the familiar voice. He took the steaming mug from Athena, trying his hardest to keep his fingers from brushing hers while maintaining a grip on the cup. He failed.

She didn't need to touch him for his body to react. But her fingers, nevertheless, brushed along his, stroking a deeper part of him that didn't awaken slowly, but roared to life without his permission. He sipped the coffee, cringing as the heat seared his lips.

"Have you seen her?" Collin asked to divert attention back to the matter on hand.

"No. She'll see only Lorraine. I heard her come in

when the taxi dropped her off. Last night Lorraine stayed in the living room waiting for her." Athena looked at the couch, but turned away quickly.

Collin refused to follow the direction of her look. All the reminders he needed were in his head and unfortunately standing a foot away from him. He wished she didn't look fresh and scrubbed clean. Her skin shone with its good health. Her hair, slightly damp, hung in loose waves to her shoulders.

"Collin, she might want to see you," Lorraine coaxed, upon entering the area.

"You're right." He headed for Cicely's room and knocked, identifying himself. He entered after hearing her weak welcome.

"Hey, kiddo."

"Uh-oh, I don't like the sound of that. You used to call me that when I first got here."

Collin nodded. "How are you doing?"

"Pride hurts. The flesh wounds will heal. And I don't feel a thing now that Dr. Singh's medicine is kicking in." Her smile wavered and her eyes pooled with tears before they crested and rolled down her face.

"You know we have to report this." Collin quickly reached for a tissue. She dabbed at her eyes. He sat on the edge of the bed holding the tissue box in easy reach.

"You can't." Cicely sobbed. "It's one of the diplomats. I didn't know the man was married. I think it was his wife who attacked me."

"Did he do anything?"

Cicely shook her head. "At first we were startled. Then when she turned her rage on me, he stepped back.

Maybe he thought it was sexy to have two women fighting over him." She blew her nose. "But I wasn't fighting. I was trying to get away. She pulled me back by my head and I fell. That's when she kicked me."

"And no one stopped this?"

Cicely sniffed. "I ran toward his house." She looked away from Collin. "Even though she attacked me in the street, no one was out there. The area was quiet." She wiped her eyes. "Then he pulled the woman, his wife, into the house and locked the door." She sniffed, wiping the tears sliding down her cheeks. "From where I stood at the bottom of the driveway, I heard them arguing. I didn't know what to do. Then a taxi pulled up."

"Where was my driver?"

"I'd sent him home. I didn't plan to come home tonight…" Her voice trailed under her shame. "But the taxi driver helped me. I'm so grateful to him."

Anger had a reason for its red color. And that's all Collin saw. He tried to remain calm and casual. "Who was the guy?"

Cicely looked at him. "I'm not telling. I can tell that you are going to do something. I don't want this in the news."

That meant it was someone with something to hide.

"No police. I mean it, Collin."

He looked down at the young lady. Now wasn't the time, but he would have to share with her the decision that he was mulling over. She would have to return home. "Get some rest."

She didn't say anything until he'd opened the door. "Please don't send me back. I can see it in your face. You're regretting that you didn't send me back when you found out that I was so young. But I didn't do anything wrong. And you'd be punishing me." Her voice grew heavy, but she fought back the drowsy state, pinning him with a woeful look.

"We'll talk when you get better."

He walked out of the room before she could protest any further. In the hallway, Athena paced. She paused when he closed the door.

"Can I go in?"

"I think she's falling asleep."

"Athena, please. Athena, come here."

Athena pushed past him and entered Cicely's room. Collin allowed them their privacy and headed to the dining area where Lorraine and Thelma sat at the dining-room table.

Lorraine motioned with her head toward the door. "I sent the guys back to their side of the world. We don't need a vigilante group to gather for vengeance."

"I agree." Collin didn't need the problem to escalate.

"Now what?" Thelma looked up at him.

"We'll allow her the time to get better."

"And then…"

"Now, Thelma, I'm not asking or receiving input on the matter." Collin didn't want to think about breaking apart his group of teachers. They were family. But this incident reminded him that he had a responsibility to them as an employer.

"You can't send her away, just like that." Lorraine snapped her fingers.

Collin got up. He had no desire to battle Lorraine or Thelma. Once Cicely was better, there would be an all-out war for what he had to recommend to the foundation. And he knew that they'd see things his way. Cicely's age had been a problem when he'd discovered that she'd lied on her résumé and was barely twenty.

"Before you think about getting rid of her, what about her class tomorrow?" Lorraine's question was heavy, laded with anger.

"Thelma and Bill can split the classes."

"Thelma is taking the smaller kids to the beach."

"Well, that will have to be postponed," Collin snapped.

"How about if I took a class? I'd love to jump right in." Athena entered the room and stood off to the side, not picking a side.

"You haven't had your orientation." Collin looked at Lorraine, although he knew that he was being unfair because the entire day's schedule had been turned upside down. "The kids need time to get to know you and get used to you."

"In a perfect world that might work." Athena took a step to where Lorraine and Thelma sat. "I'm here, ready and able to do the job. It'll give me a couple days to really get to know the children. By then Cicely will be up and around."

"Not if he plans to send her home like an inconvenient package." Thelma glared at Collin.

"You can't." Athena looked at him as if he was the bad guy. "Why? On what grounds?"

Collin shoved his hands in his pockets. "Look, Cicely knew that her time here was probationary. It doesn't mean that she did something wrong. But I've decided that her development requires more than what I can offer."

"I think the stuff you're spouting sounds like the stuff that the pigs eat." Thelma slammed down her mug.

"How about partnering me with her? She can help me get acquainted with the processes and the children. I can be a peer mentor to her," Athena suggested.

"Peer mentor?" Collin folded his arms, ready to battle the ridiculous suggestion.

Lorraine stood, mimicking his mannerisms by folding her thick arms. Thelma, sizing up the situation, quickly joined in and stood shoulder to shoulder.

"This is serious."

"We're serious. Consider us the new sorority." Athena stepped up. Her eyes held a determination that he didn't expect from her.

"Good day, ladies." He didn't want to use Cicely to make a point or to assert his position.

He could hear the rising din of confusion that his refusal to engage with them caused as their voices whispered among themselves.

"Mr. Winslow," Lorraine called out.

"So it's Mr. Winslow, now." He turned and waited.

"All we're asking is for a chance for us to make things work. Athena was the one able to calm down Cicely when she came home. It's Athena that Cicely wants. Maybe she can help her through this time. We're her family and you know this. I'd say that Athena is more than capable of handling the girls, even the difficult cases."

Collin couldn't argue with what Lorraine said. She made sense. And this solution wouldn't cause turmoil in the staff. He raised his hands in surrender. "Okay, I'll give your options a shot."

"Good." Lorraine looked triumphantly at Thelma and Athena. "Now go ahead and give Athena the orientation while I tend to dinner."

"I was doing dinner today. A Yankee BBQ. I have hot dogs, hamburgers, chicken." Collin refused to be in the same space with Athena. He couldn't control his thoughts or feelings with regard to her. Like now. She stood there with a hurt look. And he felt like the ogre.

"I've got dinner under control. Now get going before it gets too late." Lorraine shoved them both toward the door. "Thelma, start cutting up those vegetables."

"One day you're going to realize that I'm the boss."

Lorraine grunted.

Thelma laughed.

Athena had the grace to look down at her feet.

His next hire would definitely be male.

Chapter 5

Now that she had time to think about it, Athena wasn't sure that forcing Collin to keep Cicely on the staff and allowing her to teach the class was a good idea. But she always rooted for the underdog, like when she was there for her sorority sister, Denise, who had to deal with her bad gambling habits. But under this new roof, the women's unity could have consequences.

"We'll go to the office building first," he barked.

How long would he stay angry? The way he kicked the rock out of the way as he walked offered a clue that his temper might be escalating instead of heading in the other direction.

She wanted adventure, no dull routine. Seemed like her prayers were answered, just not in the way she'd imagined.

"Collin?" She entered the dark building where she'd

seen Collin enter a few seconds ahead. He'd stormed across the compound almost as if he was trying to get away from her. She reached out, feeling for the walls and any doorways. If he wanted to play these games, she'd head outdoors until he came to get her. "Collin?" She tried one last time.

The lights came on, momentarily disorienting her. She blinked until her eyes adjusted to the brightness. He stood in the doorway jangling keys.

"There is an electronic lock on the door because we have the equipment in here like the copy machine, the computer lab, sewing machines and full kitchen for home economics."

The place was clean and orderly. The air smelled faintly of disinfectant. Trash cans were empty.

She stepped into each room and surveyed the area.

"There is a connecting door to the classrooms. Again there is a lock and camera for added security."

"In one sentence you stress how safe it is, but in another way, you suggest that there is something sinister."

"Sorry about that. I want people to enjoy what we have here. Unfortunately there are the unsavory sort who try to milk everything for what they deem of value."

"I understand." Athena moved along into the hallway of the classrooms. Excitement built as she entered the classrooms that would be hers. The girls were thirteen-year-olds with a variety of family backgrounds. Poverty, however, was the one thing in common.

She stood in front of the classroom looking at the chairs and tables. Her mood lightened over the pos-sibilities. This was where she was meant to be. She looked forward to seeing the smiling faces of the eager students.

"You'll have six girls in this class. They will be our first high school students and eventual graduates. I'm working on having an established scholarship program in place."

"Where did the previous classes go?"

"Some made it into private schools. Some struggled through the government schools. Unfortunately far too many drop out." Collin sighed, his expression grim. "We've got a good library. Could be better, but we're getting more books that capture their interest."

"I plan to have them write a book at the end of the session."

"You might have to help with writing skills. A few are lacking in that area. We do have a workbook that we use."

"Not to worry. I have a few tricks that would have them writing in no time."

"Yes, but we have an approved syllabus."

Athena opened her mouth to answer. Noting the chilly difference in Collin's tone, she wisely chose to remain silent. But then she couldn't help herself. "Do you teach?"

"No. I was a counselor for a couple years." Collin adjusted a few books on the shelf. "I love the administrative side to things. The behind-the-scenes things that keep everything running. Personal reasons and the need on this island put me on the path for making this school a reality."

Athena wondered if he'd ever reveal the personal details. Sounded like they shared passion for their calling. She looked at Collin's face, pensive and brooding. While she had occasional misgivings, he appeared to be confident with his position.

"I'll be visiting your classroom throughout the probationary period."

He delivered the statement as if the probation was a fifty-pound weight he was placing on her shoulders. What if the students didn't respond to her or the parents? More important, did *he* want her gone? With his post-kiss attitude it certainly felt like it.

"I'll show you the other classrooms," he continued, interrupting her dismal thoughts.

Their progress through the remainder of the rooms should have been a fairly slow examination of the layout. Instead Collin raced through, barely giving her detailed explanations. At least Lorraine's class was situated across the hall and she was available to assist. She doubted if she would call Collin as the first option if she encountered trouble.

Deliberating over her present circumstances, she didn't know that Collin had stopped until she bumped into his back. "My fault."

"Not a problem. We've come to the end of the tour and to the history of the school."

Athena nodded, although she wasn't so agreeable that she had learned the complete history of the place. What Collin had reiterated, she had read in the school brochure.

"Wonder how Cicely is doing?" Athena looked at her watch. Only an hour had passed. But they now stood in the doorway for several seconds saying nothing to each other. Every second made the space uncomfortable.

"I have to call the police about it."

"But she didn't want any police."

"And that's not smart. And because I can't act on a

do this. I don't act this way." He held his head in his hands as if his head hurt.

Athena dressed quickly. "I don't have a habit of this either." Maybe he thought she was a floozy. But far from it, she hadn't dated much after college. Her focus on her finance career and then the switch to teaching took all of her time. Yet she didn't attribute her reaction to Collin as a binge.

"I don't think that I should stick around."

His constant denial for what had transpired irritated her. What happened wasn't ugly and to be ashamed of. She buttoned her blouse and shoved it in her pants.

"I don't think that we should be alone together. We'll try to act like responsible adults. I will observe you at your job, make recommendations. You will help Cicely along and get her back on her feet. If you need anything just let Lorraine know. She's the one responsible for training."

Athena listened and tried not to roll her eyes. How could she be attracted to this man who lived by rules? How hard would he fight his body's response, its needs? The next time, and there would be a next time, he would have to beg her for attention.

She saluted him when he finally stopped talking. He adjusted his clothing, shook his head once more and returned to his car.

Collin didn't go home right away. To sit in his living room would invite his memory to recall the sweet temptation he delved into with Athena. The woman would his downfall.

He needed something to take out his aggression.

whim and let emotion color my decision, I will talk to the police off the record. What happened to Cicely concerns Cicely, the school and the staff."

Athena listened to his no-nonsense message. His adamant announcement about his emotion and whims were like a douse of cold water. She suspected that he would involve the police, on the record. But she was afraid to ask what the punishment would be. His fury over what had happened to Cicely couldn't just evaporate.

She brushed past him with rising irritation.

Her disappointment of his not acknowledging what had transpired between them also irked her. She wasn't stupid about the ramifications. But she felt that it wasn't a mistake.

That kiss had stirred her passion into a heated brew. It had flowed through her system like hot lava.

Being completely ignored didn't sit well with her. She wanted a release for the pent-up feelings that she couldn't dismiss. She wanted more.

"We've got to talk." Collin's hand closed over her wrist, keeping her within inches of him. She rested her palm against his chest, straining to keep her body away from his. His proximity had the potential to make her melt. She didn't want to play games. The rules were too complicated.

"I want to say sorry for last night," he whispered.

"No. Please don't." Athena rested her head gently against his chin. "No regrets. It makes that moment cheap like two adults carrying on without regard."

"I don't want you to be uncomfortable because of my actions."

"Maybe you would feel better if I removed your guilt and laid it squarely at my feet."

Collin squinted; his hand relaxed its grip around her wrist. "How would you do that?"

"I would jump in with both feet." Athena hadn't planned any of this. But adrenaline coursed through her veins. Maybe it clouded her judgment. Maybe the surge to her system nibbled away at her inhibitions.

In this semidarkened spot in the hallway, she was only a few steps from emerging into the bright outdoors. To do so would kill anything on the verge of happening. The alternative would decisively shove her next action into the ever-widening chasm of guilty seduction.

That's what her body craved. One thing, one person, could satisfy her need.

She slid her hand behind his head before tiptoeing to meet his lips. Hell, it might be her last stand. She wasn't going down without a fight.

She kissed his mouth with a possessive fervor that coaxed him until she heard his guttural response. She kept up the frenzy, demonstrating that she had the stamina, power and redemption during a time when so much lay at risk.

She craved the strength of his mouth, firm, masculine, sexy and sensual. She planted kisses against his full lips, intermittently tasting him with the peppered touch of her tongue.

His restraint broke like a dam against a single-minded tide of her attention. He pushed her back against the wall, pinning her hands over her head. He leaned back, staring at her mouth as if he saw something there only for him.

While he kissed her, he pushed his thigh ___ hers. Athena pushed against his chest, but ___ still pinned hers. She groaned with frustratio___ being able to set her hands all over his body.

They warred with each other, their lips and ___ performing guerrilla warfare along each other's ___ chin and throat. But when he licked the indentatio___ her throat, she gasped and pushed off with sur___ strength. Warm sizzling feelings spiraling out of ___ blossomed between her legs, eliciting a moist rea___

He unbuttoned her shirt, flinging back each side. Without undue effort, he scooped her toward him by the small of her back. The movement raised her c___ toward his face. Her breasts anticipated his touch___ wanted to be free of the lace contraption shield___ nipples from his mouth.

He unsnapped the bra behind her back ___ slipped it off, not wanting to be bothered wi___ striction. He cupped her breasts in his palm___ his thumb against her sensitive nipples. E___ made the ache between her legs that much ___

"You drive me insane, woman."

Athena heard the agonized wail like a ___ She'd fallen into a swoon from the hyper___ had her senses in a whirl.

"I can't do this." This time Collin'___ sounded urgent, breaking the thin surfac___

The crack allowed enough reality to ___ of her ardor.

"We can't keep doing this." Collin ___ closed before turning away for her to ___

Making a tire-squealing U-turn, he headed into the downtown area. Traffic was fairly light considering it was Sunday afternoon when families would be sitting down for an early dinner, as the island culture was prone to do.

His father now resided in the States and many members of his extended family were divided among Canada and England. Distant cousins, aunts and uncles from dubious branches of the family lived on the island and the Dominican Republic. All in all, Collin had gotten used to relying on himself.

During his chaotic childhood, his mother had danced between the decision to leave his father or not. He'd dealt with the financial mess of a single parent who knew only how to be a dutiful housewife, and his father, whose aim was to get out of the country and seek a better life, no matter what. Collin had learned to protect himself and insulate his emotions from the cruelties that faced him as a child. Finally his parents had reconciled and he had a chance to experience a tranquil period until his mother's death. But he'd never trusted that his life condition would be constant. The insecurity propelled him to make certain decisions, like considering college a necessity.

Nothing came easy to him. He'd worked hard through college. His distinctions had come with long hours of studying and participating in internships all over the world. His networking abilities had landed him with the right connections so that when this project was newly created, he stepped up to lead. Many people had had to be convinced that he had the leadership skills, but he had had powerful backers who trusted in him. He'd made a promise to himself that he'd not let them down.

He headed for the police commissioner's home instead of where he'd love to go. But making dangerous deals with Kitchner's crew for retribution against Cicely's attacker was asking for trouble, no matter how tempting.

"Collin, good to see you. This is a surprise."

Collin greeted the commissioner after being led into the spacious living room by the maid. A fan whirred overhead, making the temperature comfortable. He sank into the couch as the commissioner took his seat. His cigar was poised on a nearby ashtray with a string of wispy smoke curling into the air.

"Sorry to interrupt your family time."

"I know you wouldn't be here if it wasn't important. You've been keeping yourself pretty scarce from my view." He picked up the cigar and drew upon it, filling his lungs. His piercing gaze honed in on Collin through the haze. "I know you don't always like my way of doing things."

Collin shrugged. "I had an incident with one of my teachers. One of the women."

The clarification had the necessary effect to make the commissioner set down his cigar and lean forward. He beckoned for Collin to continue.

Collin retold the story not leaving out any helpful details because he couldn't tell the important information about the identity of the man.

"That should be easy to solve. I'll check with the taxi cabs and find out where she was picked up. If the person was at the embassy party, that is another clue. These foreign types think they can manhandle women and get away with it through their immunity."

"But the guy technically didn't attack."

"Clarification isn't necessary. He'll come to understand that he acted like a punk and is an accessory. How's the young woman doing? She's the lively one, right?"

"She's shaken up. I'm on the verge of sending her back home to Vermont."

"I'd like a chance to rectify the situation. I don't want the bad press that would come from something like that. What you're doing, we all appreciate. Keeps a lot of young children off the street. Gives the parents hope." He settled back in his chair and picked up his cigar.

"Nothing crazy," Collin warned. There might be a debt to be repaid. "Let me know what you find out." Collin rose to leave.

"Will do, young man. Come back again and stay a while for dinner. We can really chat and get caught up."

Collin nodded. As long as he'd been on the island since his return, he barely visited anyone. His life was consumed with the school.

Now that he had taken care of Cicely's situation, he headed home. His stomach growling had him make a detour to a fast-food restaurant. His BBQ dinner plans had failed. And his final declaration to Athena closed the door to dinner at the school.

On most days he wouldn't have minded going back to his house and relaxing to soft music. However, his world had been shaken like a snow globe. The dizzying effects inhibited his thinking. As he drove into his driveway and parked, he wondered if Lynette was still there. Maybe she'd share his dinner and they could chat about safe subjects.

Chapter 6

The first day of work shouldn't start with thunder and lightning. The wind blew through, bending the large palm and West Indian cedar trees. Despite the hectic behavior going on outdoors and within the teachers' home, everyone bustled with their early morning routine.

"Hey, don't get nervous." Lorraine patted Athena on her back as she passed her empty coffee mug for a refill. "I'm the designated mom around here. I keep everyone in line, but I also make sure everyone has what they need to be a success."

"It's not that." Athena looked out the window at the angry gray clouds that rolled in and tightly interweaved itself into a thick blanket. "Do you think the weather is a bad sign?"

"No way. I like the rain. It washes away everything, leaving the place sparkling and green when it's over."

Athena appreciated Lorraine's upbeat viewpoint and the effort to reassure her. Maybe she would've felt better if Cicely had gotten out of bed. Instead the young woman had grown cranky and refused to budge from the bed. But lying there didn't stop Cicely from telling her how to do her job. The young woman had even extracted promises from Athena to do everything as told to her. Cicely wanted to only think about the students and their confusion over her absence.

"Ready?" Thelma lightly touched Athena on the shoulder.

Athena jumped. She shared a laugh about her nerves with the women. Taking a deep breath, she stepped out and stood on the porch, ready to take the walk. Once at the classroom building, several students had already arrived.

"They must be really eager," Athena observed.

The children came in quietly greeting every teacher they encountered, even her with a "Good morning, miss."

Lorraine looked at her watch. "In the beginning, we reiterated to their parents that the school didn't start until eight-fifteen. But every morning there would be a handful of kids who looked like they rolled out of bed and came here. We told the parents that if they got them cleaned up, wearing their uniforms, we'd be happy to serve breakfast. This is the result."

"Lorraine is tough with us, but she's a marshmallow with the children." Thelma nudged Athena when a little girl came over to Lorraine to share her jelly sandwich.

Lorraine shook her head, patted the child on the head

and said a few comforting words. The little girl's face lit up before she skipped back to join her friends.

Athena couldn't wait for the time when she would be comfortable and know the routine. With so much happening in the short period, she felt bonded to the small group of women.

Collin's truck entered the school yard. He exited the vehicle, wearing dark shades. No matter what he wore, he looked fantastic. Her eyes happily sent its critical review to the rest of her body. A quick pulse was the first side effect.

She tried not to crave the heady excitement from being close to him. But her emotions were too strong in favor of the temptation. Without looking at her, he continued his long strides into the building.

"Well, the boss man is here. Let's take our places," Thelma quipped.

Athena looked at Lorraine for an explanation. She followed her to the entrance of the school. Each teacher stood in an unmarked spot. Rows of children lined up with a teacher at the head.

The children filled in Cicely's lane but were unsettled by her absence at the front of the line. Athena stepped into the spot, displayed what she hoped would be considered a genuine smile. A few girls stopped chatting among themselves to check her out. Others ignored her, getting louder as they mutually shared their stories.

"Young ladies and gentlemen," Collin began, his voice crisp and no-nonsense over the loudspeaker. "There is a change in schedule for Miss Cicely. She is recuperating from an unfortunate mishap, but will be back in no time. We are happy to get Athena who will take Miss Cicely's classes, as well as be our home economics teacher."

Noisy chatter buzzed. The rest of the assembly consisted of announcements. Less than fifteen minutes later, Collin warned against fighting and announced the next date for parents' night.

Like Act One in a play, the curtain rose to reveal her life. She felt her calling on this island was about to be put to a test. Athena stood in front of her classroom as the children filed in quietly. There wasn't any of the madness of kids talking loudly, jostling each other or making inappropriate comments that she'd encountered back home. Instead the children moved silently down the hall. When they passed, the curiosity lit their eyes, but they said nothing.

When the last child of her class entered, Athena took a deep breath. In a few minutes, she'd have to talk. Lorraine gave her a thumbs-up from across the hall. One by one, each teacher closed the room to their class. Athena closed hers, while looking forward to meeting the girls.

"Good morning, everyone. I'm Miss Athena. Miss Cicely is not feeling well at the moment, and will be out of school for several days." Athena paused to see the effect of the news. Still there was no comment or raising of hands. Their eyes followed her from one corner of the room as she paced back and forth.

"Let's take a few minutes to get to know each other. Please tell me your names and a little bit about yourself."

Each child followed her instruction. They were

hesitant initially and the first few barely shared any personal information. Then one girl seized the opportunity. Her face grew animated and a broad smile emerged. She looked at Athena with an air of expectancy.

"Go ahead," Athena urged.

The girl stood, looking over at her peers who looked quite surprised. She cleared her throat. "Miss, I'm Marigold Fuentes. Everyone calls me Mary." Her voice dropped from its exuberance to a final note of resignation.

"But what would you like to be called?"

"Oh, miss, I'm used to Mary."

Athena saw the matter-of-factness in the small shoulders. In that young face she saw a strong spirit who intrigued her. She walked over to her more for the benefit of the class and touched her shoulder. "What would you prefer?"

"Marigold."

"Then Marigold it is. Class, from this time forward, we will address Marigold by her given name."

Silence reigned.

"Is there an objection?" This time Athena looked at each girl for a full second.

"No, miss," the class replied in unison.

Athena looked at Marigold and nodded. The girl beamed.

"Is there anything else you'd like to add to your introduction, Marigold?"

"I am new to the school. I've been here one month." The young girl lowered her head and then her body wilted and she took her seat.

"Looks like you're no longer new, Marigold. Now

I'm the new one. In America, my nickname would be 'newbie.'"

The girls giggled. And Marigold looked relieved. With her thick braids and big, brown eyes, she reminded Athena of herself.

Athena didn't have to dig deep in the memory banks to know how difficult fitting in could be. As an adult, she didn't think the process was much different. She could at least be thankful that she gained inner strength to deal with people's cruelty. The disadvantage to being a twin came with the curiosity and attention people gave her. Adolescent jealousy and envy served up lots of nastiness in high school.

At that moment, she looked up from the textbook in her hand. Collin stood in the hallway staring at her. His expression was difficult to discern, although happiness at seeing her didn't come to mind.

If he meant to intimidate, she wasn't biting. This was her classroom. Temporary or not, she had to lead and push away her fears about what he thought and wrote in his folder.

"Please open your books to page one hundred. Each student will read a paragraph until I tell you to stop. I will ask questions that come directly from the essay. There might be a grade or there might not. You will have to pay attention."

The collective groan hovered over the room before dying abruptly.

Collin stepped fully into the classroom.

Athena paused to see if he had something important to say. His presence almost obstructed her ability to teach, Athena stepped into the line of his scrutiny. Keeping her back to him, she clapped her hands to return the children's attention to her.

"Please begin." She nodded to the first girl in the far left corner. The girl twirled her hair, staring down at the page.

Athena waited, understanding her nervous state. The girl scooted forward in the chair, opened her book and began to read.

One at a time, each girl read a paragraph. When Marigold had to read, she stared at the page, looked up at Athena and then burst into tears.

A giggle erupted from the back of the classroom. Athena's sharp gaze sliced through the room to the spot where she suspected the student to be seated. Her students had to learn fast that she had zero tolerance for such behavior.

With Marigold sobbing, Athena hesitated with focusing her attention on Marigold or taking the impolite student to task. Before she could decide, Collin headed to the suspect heckler. Now the students were not only silent, but eerily still. Like wax dolls, they stared ahead, posture rigid. Only their luminous eyes expressed the wariness of dreaded anticipation.

Students scared at one end, Collin barged in at the other end. And she stood in the middle, losing her influence and authority in a matter of seconds. Collin trampled over any inroads she'd made.

"Abigail, please come forward." Collin moved farther down the aisle until he was at the desk. Not until the girl answered did he return to the front of the room.

Slowly the girl walked.

"Stella Maris has strict rules of conduct, correct?"

"Yes, sir."

"Would you please repeat the three central values?"

"Do unto others as you would have them do unto you. Be respectful at all times. Being a bully is no better than being a coward." Abigail's voice dropped at each sentence, along with her head, as she now looked at her feet.

"Class, did you hear that?"

"Yes, sir," the class answered.

Collin stared at each girl. Then he turned to Athena. "You should have no problem with the remainder of the time." Then he exited the room without another glance.

Constructive criticism was one thing. Being usurped for no reason other than controlling issues was something entirely different. But there would be a time to address the issue.

"Abigail, you may take your seat. Let's continue. Sarita, please read. It's your turn."

The session continued without further incident. Three students needed extra help with reading. Athena talked to them as a group, offering to help them during their one-hour lunch break, starting at the beginning of the following week. She reminded them to tell their parents.

The girls looked enthusiastic, except for Marigold. Deciding not to push the matter, Athena resisted questioning the girl for the time being.

Despite the shorter school day, the time felt laden with more attention on individual needs. She looked forward to the lunch break, sitting in a chair, falling into a state of exhaustion.

"Hey, why don't you head back to the house and put

up your feet for a few minutes." Lorraine stuck her head in the classroom.

"I can't. I should eat with the girls."

"Sorry to pop your balloon, but the girls won't want you sitting with them. Gives them time to talk about us."

Athena shared the laugh. "Then maybe I need to eat with the other teachers. You know, I have to bond."

"Look, unless you're planning to catch the next plane out—and there will be times you'll feel that way—go get your head together. Don't let these children know that you don't have the stamina."

Athena nodded. "I won't be long."

Lorraine waved at her and left.

Athena looked around the empty classroom, desperately trying to squelch the feeling that she had taken on more than she could deal with. Her biggest fear was that her input wouldn't make a difference. A small number of teachers battling against poverty and old mind-set from the parents gave the impression of a challenging walk up a steep mountain. Fear unsettled her. But maybe she had too much arrogance to think that she could be like her grandmother. She rotated her shoulders, trying to loosen the tension locked from her neck, radiating out to each shoulder. Appreciating Lorraine's advice, she opted to multitask and kick up her feet. With the first grading assignment under her arm, she headed to the house trying to shake the guilt of leaving her peers and her students.

The house was a bit warm under the midday sun. Ceiling fans whirred noiselessly. Hopefully the place wasn't unbearable for Cicely. After knocking and announcing herself, she entered the room.

Cicely played solitaire on her bed, barely looking at her entrance. The usual vibrant attitude that had been her trademark had disappeared. The blond hair needed washing. The pallor of her skin looked nothing like the suntanned, carefree woman. Her eyes also appeared pale.

"I'm scared, Athena."

"About what, sweetie?"

"That Collin will send me home."

Athena smoothed away the loose hair from her face.

"Don't you worry about that. All of us convinced him to back off."

"Really?"

"You need to come out of this room. Then you'll see firsthand how much people miss you."

"You're like my angel."

"And you're like my little sister, if I had one."

Athena got a glass of lemonade and a ham sandwich before heading for the porch. From the front of the house, she had a direct view of the covered, open area where everyone sat for lunch. She walked to the side of the building for more privacy.

A white wicker lounge chair, a hammock and a single chair were her furniture choices. The upright chair didn't appeal to her, but the hammock was at the other extreme. Besides she wasn't sure that she could get in without the hammock flipping over and depositing her onto the floor. And there was no elegant way that she knew how to get in and get out. The lounge chair won.

She eased herself into position, kicking off the shoes with kitten heels. She wiggled her burgundy nail-polished toes, stretching her foot and relaxing it, while emitting a sleepy yawn.

The voices from the school area drifted softly through the air. She slid down against the headrest, planning to enjoy the island breeze for about five minutes. Then she should feel refreshed to get to the papers that needed grading. Athena crossed her legs at the ankles, folded her fingers over her stomach and listened to the rhythmic pattern of the waves against the coastline.

With a small staff and student population, Collin didn't think that he should have any problem locating Athena. Yet after searching the classrooms and the common area, he couldn't find her.

"Lorraine, Thelma, have you seen Athena?"

"She's taking a breather." Lorraine took a bite out of her sandwich, motioning toward the house with her head.

"Is there a problem?" Collin looked at his watch, seeing that she had forty-five minutes remaining for her breather. Teachers didn't have the luxury of nap time in the States. He hoped she wasn't planning to take advantage.

"It's her first day, Collin. Remember how we all were," Thelma chimed in.

"It may be her first day here, but she's an experienced teacher." Collin readjusted his shades. He didn't care if these women wanted to frown at him. His job didn't allow for friends. It was all about the children.

"Collin, she'll be fine. Give her a break. We need her," Lorraine urged.

Instead of responding, he turned and headed toward the women's house. Before Cicely's incident, he hadn't planned on using Athena as a solo teacher. Her orientation was supposed to be a gradual one. But that was in an ideal world. And around here, ideal, or even normal, was far from reach some days.

The porch ahead of him was empty. He walked up to the door and knocked. Several seconds passed before the door opened.

"Cicely, what are you doing out of bed?"

She waved him away, partially covering her bruised face with her other hand.

"Sorry to bother you." He shifted about, not sure what to do. Every time he thought about her and what happened, he wanted to punch someone's face in. "Are you in pain?" He winced.

"Not really. But I'm still a bit woozy on my feet."

"Go back to bed. I was looking for Athena."

"Maybe she's in her room. I'll check." She opened the door farther, inviting him.

He glanced around, marveling at the tidiness of their house compared to the men's house.

Cicely stepped out of the room. "Don't see her. Maybe she went back to the classrooms."

Collin looked back at the school, wondering if he'd missed her. He wasn't giving up his search.

"Collin, I really want to stay here."

"I know, Cicely. And you've got Athena in your corner."

"She told me that, but I can tell that I don't have *you* in my corner."

"But you do. More than you will ever know." Collin looked away, not wanting anyone to know that he had relied on his connections with Ambassador Piedmont to eject a man and his wife off the island or risk the locals' wrath. He lightly touched her face.

"I've been putting ice on my face." She turned so he could see the progress of her healing.

However, the blackness had a yellow tinge and was still swollen. The doctor had visited this morning, but only said that she was on the mend. Her discoloration made his knees weak.

"In a day or so, I can use makeup to hide it."

"Whatever you need, Cicely." He turned to leave, but a flash of color fluttering in the breeze caught his eye. "You go rest, okay?" He waited until she'd retired to her room before turning back to what had captured his attention.

As he approached the window, he saw Athena's still form in the lounge chair. Not the position that he envisioned, but he found it disturbingly preferable. He climbed out of the low window, resting his frame against the windowsill.

Serene was the only way to describe her. Again long legs. The swell of her breasts. The calmness of her features punctuated by a provocative mouth. Her skin color.

He couldn't withstand the temptation to linger over the beauty of her body, especially those legs. Her soft brown skin glistened flawlessly, tempting him as if he could take his finger and scoop a dollop of caramel. And when he could resist no longer, he admired every nuance and curve of her mouth. He sat back enjoying the precious moments afforded him to admire openly.

Unfortunately a loud island bird gave its piercing whistle. A frown crossed her forehead and then she stirred. Collin tried to slip back into the window, but ended up bumping his head, emitting a loud grunt.

"Oh!" Athena's eyes opened wide, alarm blazing through her mortified gaze. She hurriedly swung her legs off to the side of the chair, alternating between smoothing her hair and clothes in the process.

"Sorry…I came to look for you." Collin debated whether he should sit or stand.

"What time is it? Didn't mean to fall asleep. The air. The place." Athena stopped talking; she worked at her bottom lip.

"You're not late. I only wondered if you were okay."

"I'm fine." Athena stood and picked up a set of papers that were tucked under her leg. "I'd better be going."

Collin nodded. He wasn't prepared for her to leave, but he had no reason to delay her.

She had descended the stairs when she turned back. "One thing…"

"Sure."

"Please don't interrupt my classroom again. Just like you're doing to me, the girls are also trying me out. The slightest sign of weakness doesn't help my cause. If you have a problem in the way I'm doing something, then we can talk about it later."

"Then don't give me cause to step in and take control." Collin hadn't expected this reaction.

Athena looked as if she had more to say. He stood

and walked toward her. She could think what she wanted about his methods, but he was the boss.

"I hope this isn't about you and me. About…well, you know…" She wiped her mouth, which only drew his attention to her lips' softness.

"In no way am I linking our mutual misbehavior to my role as school administrator and as your boss." He shoved any memories of her body against his, raising his senses with sensual thoughts and inappropriate images.

"Misbehavior, is it?" A smirk lifted the edge of her mouth. She sauntered off.

Collin didn't view their short relationship as combative, but he did feel as if he'd lost a point with this last exchange. Her smug reaction to his role didn't sit well with him. That smile was enough to incite him to remove it.

While she walked toward the classrooms, he chose the opposite direction and headed for his office. With tons of paperwork on his desk, he could be occupied for several hours. But contrary to what she desired, he would continue watching her every move.

The first week passed with no further intervention necessary. Collin still monitored Athena's progress, sometimes making his presence felt and, other times, getting Lorraine's or Thelma's feedback. From everything he observed and the reports he received, Athena displayed the great strengths that he'd expected from her résumé.

Yet he had a few reservations that she may not be diplomatic when necessary. He wanted a softer touch with the families. Not everyone appreciated Athena having their child stay behind for tutoring. And whenever he introduced the possibility of his being the negotiator with the family, she refused his help.

He packed his briefcase, heading for home. His father, a widower, was flying in for a week. Although he didn't really have a lot of time to spend with him, his father made a trip to the island twice a year.

He visited in July because his mother died that month from a stroke, and in October because that's when they were married.

Collin tried to suggest other months, but his father wouldn't budge. After ten years since his mother's death, he came to realize that his father needed to do this as part of his grieving.

"Clarissa, I'm heading out for the day. If anyone needs me, I'll be at home."

"Ivan is coming in this evening?"

Collin nodded. His assistant had been flirting with his father since the school opened during his visit. However, his father was completely clueless to her attempts. Collin didn't like playing matchmaker, especially with employees.

"I hope he pops in tomorrow." She picked up her small compact and flipped it open.

"Can't promise anything."

She primped in the mirror, smoothing down her eyebrows and then removing the excess lipstick from her mouth. She snapped the mirror shut. "I'll be ready whenever he gets here."

Collin took his briefcase and headed for the car. Nothing about this place lent itself to make him believe in people falling in love. From his point of view, the place represented a lofty ambition to teach and educate the future generation, nothing more.

"Mr. Winslow! Mr. Winslow!"

Collin hit the brakes. The security guard pointed to something or someone behind his car. He looked up at the rearview mirror. He stuck his head out the window.

The sight behind him alarmed him. Clarissa's short, stocky body shuffled in a quick step, waving at him. The security men were also beckoning him to follow. Collin emerged from his car, not guessing at what could be the problem.

"Please come quickly," Clarissa urged, breathless from the exertion.

Collin broke into a run. "What is it?"

"It's the new teacher and Marigold's mother."

"What?"

"Marigold's mother, Luisa, is furious. I think she might punch Athena."

Collin didn't wait to hear any more details. Instead he turned up the speed and headed for the classroom. As he got near the building, he heard the raised voice of Luisa. She had a reputation for being hotheaded. The others had faced the woman's fiery disposition and knew how to defuse the situation.

Athena's responses seemed to be inciting Luisa into a fury. He hurried down the hallway, wondering why Luisa was here in the first place. School had been over for an hour. He opened the classroom door.

Athena was making a point, holding up one finger, then two, and now three. Luisa, on the other hand, had a vein raised in her neck as she screamed a string of curses in Spanish. Her hands were firmly planted on her hips—a good sign, so far.

They both looked up at him. Neither looked happy to see his appearance. He took a deep breath and forced himself to stay cool and calm and be willing to play King Solomon.

Chapter 7

Drama in her life was in full supply. Athena dreaded the sudden appearance of Collin followed by Clarissa and the other teachers. Their stares fastened on her. Why should she expect anything better? *The new teacher had screwed up once again.* Her best intentions had sparked a war. All she'd suggested was to make herself available to tutor Marigold. Maybe she'd have to try a different approach.

"Mrs. Fuentes, I understand your goals for your daughter. Marigold had shown so much potential that I thought it was a good idea to teach her beyond what is in the class."

"Filling her head with nonsense is a waste of time. She's old enough to earn an income now."

"She can be more than a maid. She can be anything that she wants to be."

"She's my child."

"Mrs. Fuentes, I know that and respect your position. I only wanted to give her options."

"Now that you've filled her head, I won't be able to get her to accept her life."

Collin cleared his throat. "I can try."

"No, you've done enough." Marigold's mother swung her attention to Collin when he stepped into the room. "You promised me that you wouldn't interfere with my family. I may not have a husband and a fancy house. But I have to do what I have to do to keep the little roof over our head. Every minute that Marigold is here is a minute away from earning money on the big island. I need her to bring in money."

Athena was quite willing to stand there until the sun set to prove her point. Marigold had so much potential that Athena hurt not being able to go full blast with passing on knowledge.

"Everything will be all right, Mrs. Fuentes. I'm sure Athena has your child's best interest at heart." He reached for her hands and looked earnestly in her face. "Look, Marigold has shown great potential in her math and science classes. Her reading needs improvement. But I feel sure that she can get the student voucher to attend a private high school. We need all the time available to strengthen her skills. And as a crucial part of the team, we need your cooperation."

She opened her mouth to respond. But Collin cupped her hand in his before she uttered a word.

"Trust me." He kept her within inches of his face.

"I'll trust you." She looked at Athena with an entirely different expression.

Athena clasped her hands in front of her. She felt useless and embarrassed that, once again, Collin entered the fray to set things straight. Her teaching skills had never been a question in her mind, but in this unique environment clearly there was a lot for her to learn.

She observed Collin walking out with Mrs. Fuentes. His hand still covered hers. Her shoulders drooped from the release of tension after the woman left. Now that Collin had stepped in, she surmised that in a few minutes, he'd summon her to his office for the official dress down.

Athena bit her lip, welcoming the pain, rather than give in to the tears ready to introduce her self-pity party. She moved around the room, collecting work to be graded that evening.

She sighed. Everything had been going so well. Once again she'd stepped knee deep into a big mess.

"Athena, got a minute?" Collin had returned without Mrs. Fuentes.

"Sure." She wished that she could answer in the negative.

"I'd like to take you somewhere for about an hour."

"Where?" She stopped in her tracks, unsure about what Collin wanted and how she should respond. For all she knew, he wanted to take her to the airport.

"I want to introduce you to the lives of some of the students. You've seen them on our turf, but I think it's important to see them in their neighborhoods." He paused. "Interested?"

Athena nodded, still not convinced that she wasn't going to get a dressing down from Collin.

She followed him out the building to his car instead of the truck. The close confines placed her inches away from Collin. If it wasn't humid, she'd request the windows to be opened. Instead she had to deal with the soft scent of Collin's cologne. She adjusted the vents to allow the air conditioner to cool the effects of sitting next to him.

"We're going to drive to the center of the island. This is the largest poor area that a lot of the residents have deep-seated ties no matter where they move. Many move from the middle provinces to the seaside villages for work in the hotels or access to the ships that come in."

Athena nodded. She visibly cringed.

"Don't let the narrow roads scare you. I've been climbing this mountain for many years." He pushed a button and opened her window. "You can get a good look at the valley below and the numerous cattle farms and cane fields."

"This island is so lush. And the various shades of greens are really refreshing." She breathed in the smell of the rolling hills. "I'm looking forward to getting around to sightsee."

"Make sure you go with someone."

She nodded. He'd get no argument from her. Cicely's situation made everyone cautious, even overly so.

They rounded a sharp curve in the road, barely missing stray goats eating grass. Athena dug her fingers into the dashboard to steady herself. She looked over to Collin, who looked unfazed.

"We're entering the Spanish side." Collin pointed to a faded wooden sign that could have stated anything.

Immediately Athena noticed the little brightly colored houses separated by fences. The neighborhoods were a mixture of concrete two-story homes and then fell away to wooden structures. A few were made out of the metal sheets in a ramshackle way.

Roosters strolled around the various yards, lording over their domains. Bands of scrawny dogs barked at the car roaring through the area. Even the people didn't seem glad to see them.

"Don't be alarmed. Most folks around here know about the school."

"But they don't look thrilled to see you." Athena fought the urge to hit the lock.

"Some think of me as little more than a traitor because I left here, studied in the States, had a life before returning. I have been accused of being an elitist."

"I'm sure some are happy to have you come home to help them," Athena offered, noting the sad note in his declaration.

They turned down a side street, heading deeper into the dismal surroundings. Half-naked boys ran down the street, trying to keep pace with their progress.

Finally Collin pulled up in front of a house. The wood had been painted a bright yellow, but now the faded color peeled away from the structure. Despite the sad appearance, frilly white curtains blew out of the windows.

"It's Marigold's house."

"Oh." They had been driving for thirty minutes.

"How in the world does Marigold get to the school earlier than most?"

"Our major problem is transportation. I'm trying to get a designated school bus that will enable pickup and drop-off for anyone on the island who wants to come to our school."

"Do the kids use public transportation?"

"For the most part, they use buses, taxis and, in some cases, they would use a bus and still have to walk a couple miles. Guess it shows that they really want to be at the school."

"Yes, they do. They appreciate what you're offering."

Collin stared at her, then exited the car.

They walked up to the door, but it opened before they got there. Luisa Fuentes stared down at them.

"Mrs. Fuentes, I wanted to show Athena the surroundings and beauty of the island. But I also wanted you to meet Athena…really get to know her. She needs you to trust her and trust in what she's doing."

Luisa stood with her legs apart, arms crossed at her chest. Her loud lipstick color had been removed. She was dressed in a housedress and ragged slippers. Athena couldn't recall seeing the woman smile, and wondered if they would be welcomed into the house.

Marigold emerged from the shadows to stand next to her mother. The resemblance was uncanny—younger version and not-so-young version. While Luisa had dyed her hair a honey blond, Marigold's hair was still a natural chocolate brown, healthy and thick.

"Hi, Marigold," Athena greeted her. She wished that she'd known Collin's plan. There was no way that she would've agreed to come here and be stared down by the mother's hostile countenance.

"Marigold, go finish your work." Her mother's tone held no room for opposition.

"Mrs. Fuentes, this is very important," Collin coaxed.

"Fine. I'll talk to Athena—is that your name? You, on the other hand, can go take the clothes that Marigold washed to the big house on Hammons Hill on the French side. It's due in the next hour."

"Sure."

"Wait a minute. I need to talk to Collin." Athena pushed Collin back into the yard, heading to the opening that once had a gate. "What do you think you're doing?" She forced herself not to shout.

"I think this will help."

"How? Why? This woman can barely tolerate me."

"I didn't plan this, but now that I've committed, I think that it will make a difference. I got her to calm down and give you a chance. And that's because I believed in what you're doing. But you have to take the baton and do your own thing."

Athena let go of his arm as her emotions settled. Why did he have to make sense when she was convinced that he didn't know what he was doing? That he was over his head. She took a deep breath and headed back to the pinched, stern figure of Luisa.

"Marigold, get the clothes so Mr. Winslow can take them to the Bouviers. You can go with him. I need to talk to your teacher."

Athena entered the tiny living room and took a seat

in the corner. Not until Collin and Marigold left did Luisa transfer her attention to her.

"So what do you think?" Luisa threw up her hands and looked around the room.

"A very nice home." Athena didn't want to play stupid with this woman. She had a shrewdness that life had caused. "Is Marigold your only child?"

"No. She's my only child with her father, Pepe. But he decided to go back to his wife."

"Oh."

"I'm not Mrs. Fuentes. Never have been. I used it to give Marigold peace of mind. I don't really care what people think."

"I understand."

Luisa stopped her fidgeting and sized up Athena. "Stay here. I'll be back."

Athena shrugged. As if she was really going to go anywhere. Collin had unceremoniously dumped her in the middle of the island on the side of a mountain in a home of a woman who studied her like a specimen. No, she had no choice but to stay put and say her silent Hail Marys.

"I brewed tea." Luisa appeared with a steaming cup.

In the humid heat, a hot drink wasn't the ideal choice. But this wasn't the time to be difficult. Athena reached for the teacup and saucer.

"I have honey."

"Thank you." Athena spooned in the honey and sipped the liquid. She didn't know the various flavors of tea, but there was a light, fruity smoothness that she found refreshing, even if drinking the beverage ignited her internal furnace. She wiped her brow.

"You're the first teacher that I'm meeting this way."

"Really?" From the impassioned way that Collin spoke, she'd assumed that all the teachers had been brought before Luisa Fuentes and any other parents who had doubts about the school.

"He's talked highly of your skills." Luisa sipped her tea. Her dark, almost black, eyes observing, processing, very intuitive. "Marigold said you've been here for a week. And what you've done with her in five days is impressive. She now thinks that she wants to be a lawyer, a doctor, even a teacher." Luisa laughed.

"I'm glad to hear that." Athena meant it. "I want to open up their minds to possibilities. Life starts with dreams and hopefully I can give her the skills and drive to make goals and turn it into reality."

"What about those who won't go any further in their lives than as a maid or prostitute? That is common around here." Luisa leaned forward. "Collin is working by himself. No one cares about what he's doing."

"I can't guarantee that I can change each child's life. But I've been hired to give equal access to education and that's what I'm doing. And with regard to Collin, I don't believe that no one cares. There is no reason for the government to grant him the permit, the visas for the staff and the location for teaching the children if they didn't want it to be successful."

"Collin is from a connected family. When this fails, he may be out a few dollars, but he gets to go back to his cushy lifestyle. And as for that land, the government didn't give it to him. It doesn't belong to the government."

Athena drained her teacup and wanted to ask for more. This conversation had taken a turn and become more interesting. Hopefully Collin would be gone for another half hour. She didn't know if Lorraine and Thelma knew all this info on their boss.

"Collin got the location from our local, resident drug dealer."

"He mentioned a little about the circumstance."

"Everyone around here knows that."

Athena tried not to think about her new home in its true light.

"Hey, don't worry. He probably had to do it to keep them off his back. They tend to have their hands in everything on the island."

"Why do the people tolerate them?"

"Well, when you figure out how to separate the bad guys from the good guys, from those who just want to live their lives, let me know." Luisa held up the teapot for seconds. Athena nodded.

The two women continued chatting, relaxing their guards and enjoying each other's company.

"Did you leave any man back home?"

Athena shook her head.

"Why would a young girl like you get deposited on this piece of land? There had to be other viable islands that needed your service with a good supply of bachelors."

"Blame it on my desire to do something worthwhile with my life. My grandmother recently died after a long fulfilling life. Teaching runs in the family. I used to work in the financial industry but got out of that because greed didn't sit well with me."

"Don't you want a family? I know that I'm not a stellar example of family and stability, but I have no regrets."

"It hasn't crossed my mind," Athena lied, but pushed aside her conscience. She didn't know Luisa from an hour ago. How could she talk about her most intimate feelings?

Seeking the company of a man or defining her worth by a man wasn't going to happen. Athena had had casual relationships at college. And now out of university, there were the Happy Hour invites or trolling the bars for a sexy guy. But no one had managed to really capture her interest. She didn't feel hopeless. Instead she focused on her career.

"I can see from your face that I've crossed the line with you." Luisa laughed. "My mother used to be so uptight about sex. She wouldn't talk and I couldn't ask. I went elsewhere for my lessons in life. Now I've learned to say what I want." She sat back in the chair when the door opened. "You should try it sometime."

"We're back." Marigold took a seat next to her mother.

"And if you need a place to think about it, go to the Falls."

"The Falls?" Athena asked.

"*Fontaine de Jeune*. Fountain of Youth," Marigold piped up.

"It's on the French side. It's a wonderful place to clear the head." Luisa placed an arm around her daughter's waist.

"Mr. Winslow is waiting in the car," Marigold reported.

Athena had wondered where he was. She hurriedly thanked Luisa for the tea and more important the tentative branch of friendship. Having entered the house with trepidation, she now exited with a lighter mood.

The first week had rolled through with lots of bumps and bruises. Since then, life had taken a turn for the consistent, heading toward one month under her belt. Although the classes with the girls were going along in a healthy clip, the chance to be alone with Collin wasn't happening.

After the trip to Luisa's home, he had made no further offers to show her the island. But that didn't stop her from hopping on an island tour bus when she got the opportunity to visit the three major provinces. Bit by bit, she grew more comfortable and ready to call this place home for the near future. She was sure her sorority sisters noticed the change of heart in her long letters to them.

"Hey, what are you doing out here? We're planning to hit the movies again." Cicely plopped down next to Athena.

"Writing to my sister. I really miss her. I'm hoping that she can come and visit."

"How old is your sister?"

"She's my twin. Asia is her name. This is the first time that we've been apart for such a long time. I'm used to her being there listening to my rants." She looked over to Cicely. "How about yourself? Siblings?"

"Yeah. I have four sisters." She laughed at Athena's

surprise. "We drove our parents crazy. Then after my parents divorced, I decided that it was time for me to work out my own life's plan. I'm the third. The divorce was ugly. And my youngest sister was in the middle of a custody battle. I was given the option by the judge because I was almost an adult. I chose to stay with my mother, mainly to help her with my sister. But I couldn't handle the anger and bitterness. My little sister ended up going to live with our eldest sister. Our mother is living with my grandparents and is enrolled in a day program because of her depression."

"Wow." Athena had gotten closer to Cicely. She treasured the woman's friendship. "Do you write?"

"We exchange an e-mail or two." She pointed to the pink-colored stationery in Athena's hand. "I'm not a letter type of person."

"I like writing e-mails. But sometimes I enjoy writing a letter the old-fashioned way because it's more personal. It frees my mind and my emotions. It's sort of like a gift that I'm presenting."

"That's sweet." Cicely gave her back a comforting rub. "I'll let you get back to your sister. I'm going to head out with the others."

Athena nodded. She enjoyed the quiet as everyone went their separate ways to spend the weekend. After she wrote the letter, she folded the paper and stuffed it in the matching envelope.

The TV didn't interest her nor did sitting on the porch with a book. In her room, she opened her drawer and pulled out her swimsuit. Luisa's advice about going to the waterfall hadn't slipped her mind. Finding enough time to while away at a waterfall hadn't happened, until today.

Grabbing the keys to one of the school vans, Athena jumped in with a small basket of goodies and beach towel. With the map opened on the passenger seat, she started on her way to the place that promised to provide her answers about life.

"*Fontaine de Jeune,* here I come."

Chapter 8

Athena followed the winding trail that paralleled the coastline. On one side, the ocean rolled onto the sandy beach. On the other side of the road, the rocky landscape rose sharply. Finally she saw signs to the destination and took the turn as directed.

No one else appeared to be visiting the area. No cars had passed her for the past mile. The trees grew long and straight, towering over her with lush, verdant foliage. She looked up through the windshield, feeling comfortable that at least she could view the sky.

She approached the edge of a large opening, a parting of the thick forest very much like a biblical parting. The waterfall, the centerpiece of natural wonder, crashed over layers of rocks until it emptied into a lake. Athena stopped the car, not waiting one more minute to enjoy the beauty. The beauty had to be admired close and without the obstruction of a windowpane.

The terrain roughened with large boulders jutting up from the ground and tree roots that curled from their base. Athena walked ahead, turning in a complete circle to take in the panoramic view. Ahead was the fresh-water lake.

"This is so damn beautiful!" She threw up her hands to the sky, too overcome with what a small part she played in nature's garden.

The water glistened under the sunlight as if diamonds floated on its surface. She pulled out her brochure to read about this body of water. The locals considered the water to have healing powers, a place for rejuvenation, a place to renew the spirit. Scientists had carried out various tests on the waters, not sure how the quality remained pure.

Athena was game to find out if the findings were true. She surveyed the area, already deciding that she'd take a dip in the water. Not that she had anything physically wrong to be healed. Well, if she counted that her thoughts couldn't stop circling around one man. But she needed more than sparkling water to assist with that problem. She needed the chutzpah to go after what she wanted.

Nothing could convince her that Collin wasn't interested. She was sure that's why he went out of his way to stay away from her.

She wound her way along the edge of the lake. Following the creek to a quieter spot away from the strong current near the waterfall, she discovered a cove where the water gently rolled toward a small sandy beach.

A deafening clap of thunder ripped through the air. A rain shower in the middle of the day wasn't unusual. The downpour came without warning. The shower felt as if someone took a bucket and emptied its contents until everything was drenched. She was used to the unpredictable nature of the rain showers and didn't mind the soaking. In a few minutes, she planned to be shoulder deep in the water.

Without debating the action, she peeled off her clothes, spreading them on a nearby rock. After the rain, she expected that the strong sun would emerge and dry her clothing in no time. If not, she'd have to squish her way back to the house, happy nonetheless.

Another crack of thunder announced another deluge of warm rain. After the stickiness of the heat, she welcomed the water's cleansing power. Her hair pasted against her scalp and along her back where it hung below her shoulders. The raindrops coming in fast succession massaged her skin, raising her level of sensitivity. She cupped her hands, gathering as much of the water as she could, before bathing her face. Repeating this ritual was her small token of appreciation for entering this surreal existence.

Blocking out the world beyond this jungle and the rat race that she escaped from, Athena centered her spirit to be in tune with her surroundings. Raindrops ran over her body. Like long tantalizing fingers, they tickled her nipples through the swimsuit top.

The pool of water beckoned her. She willingly answered its bidding while the rain continued to lavish her with attention. She waded in, sucking in her breath from the water's cool temperature. In one move, she dived into the water to keep from retreating into the warm air. After a few seconds, her body acclimated and she emerged from the depths for fresh air.

The rain had ceased and the sun did indeed break through the clouds. The rays beamed down through the large opening and turned the surface of the lake into a shimmering cover.

Athena floated on her back, enjoying the heat on the full length of her body. She fluttered her legs, pushing her body toward the middle of the lake. Water had always relaxed her. And now she could understand why others thought the water had special powers.

In this state, close to nature, she had no choice but to reflect inwardly. And the person who came to mind was a tall, dark man who had a smile that brightened her day, a body that made hers perk up, and a sexy charm that stirred a craving in her that wanted satiation.

As she drifted on her back in this tropical Eden, her thoughts also drifted to where she was a year ago and how far she'd come. Her thankless job as a loan officer carried long hours. From the banking industry to teaching, she had large classes, poorly funded programs and demanding administrators who had to be concerned with politicians' agendas.

A blur of movement interrupted her thoughts. She stayed quiet, waiting. Then a blur of color that didn't blend showed through surrounding bush. Her heart pumped, frightened.

Athena shifted position, treading the water. She turned to examine what caught her eye. Not getting any resolution, she swam toward the edge. The solitude of her oasis provided a false sense of security. Now that a possible intruder threatened her space, her solitary trek didn't seem like a good idea.

Finally she regained footing in the shallow water. Nothing appeared out of the ordinary. Yet she sensed that someone remained hidden. Regardless she didn't feel comfortable and made her way to the shore. Her body tensed for an emergency flight, if necessary. A deeper feeling of unease ran through her upon noticing that the birds had quieted. Gingerly, she headed toward her towel.

"What are you thinking? Coming here by yourself. And then swimming in next to nothing."

Athena screamed and ran. Her heart pounded, as sheer terror rushed through her veins. She got to the car but then fumbled with the handle. Looking up to see where the intruder was, she suddenly stopped.

Collin stood where she was only moments ago. His hands were shoved casually in the shorts he wore. His mouth drew tight in its familiar irritable line. Once again he was about to lecture her.

She wrapped the towel around her body, took a deep breath and walked toward him. "Why are you sneaking up on me? Do you have a habit of stalking?"

"Don't be presumptuous. I have a habit of looking for you when you go traipsing off without letting anyone know."

"Then how did you find me, Sherlock?" Her heart still hadn't returned to a normal pace. She lashed out to keep the jitters away. If she let him see her frazzled, she suspected he would use it to drive home some silly point.

"You're not exactly looking native, especially in the school van. What if someone had followed you up here? And why are you here? There are better beaches and lakes than this place."

Athena had no intention of telling him about Luisa's advice. No way. She'd never seen him so angry. Even his nostrils flared as he blew out his frustration.

"If you're going to keep yelling at me, I'm heading back."

"Do you accept that what you did was stupid and careless?"

This man was a pain. She couldn't stand the cocky way he tilted his head, looking down at her. Always ready with his superior attitude, he looked the part even in his ridiculous khaki shorts.

"The only thing I'm planning to accept is the fact that you can't go one day without thinking about me." When he recoiled, she took a step closer. "Not only do you think about me, but you have to see me." She continued walking toward him. "But it's okay because I want to see you, too." She dropped the towel. "I want you to touch me."

"You are a brazen woman."

"And I'm waiting for a man who doesn't hide behind a lot of useless insights."

"Don't start something—"

"Oh, I can finish. The real question is whether you've got what it takes to stay the course until I'm done…with you."

"Why couldn't you just be a normal teacher?"

"That's a matter of perspective."

Collin looked at Athena's eyes glittering with her

anger. He'd followed her because he wanted to take her to the local steel band festival occurring that evening. Not that this was a special occasion, but he knew that she hadn't gone with the others to the movies. By the time he'd headed to the school, he'd barely seen the van speed down the road in a cloud of dust.

Watching her now take off her clothes and head into the water, he almost lost any self-control. He couldn't deny that he was indeed interested in Athena and not as her boss. She was a constant temptation that he found difficult to resist. There was no way that he could allow his staff to detect that there was any interest with her. The workplace could not be a place for bad behavior.

"You are so far from normal that you'd need a guide to help you back to that point," he remarked.

"Looks like you have dibs on that job." She threw her towel over his head. "I'm going for another swim. You can stay there like a statue and scare away the bad guys."

Collin pulled the towel down from over his head. The last view of Athena was of her running toward the water. Her soft brown skin showed off the tangerine-orange bikini.

She turned toward him and waved. "Forget the rules for a little while. No one is here. Come on. You know you want to."

Collin bit down on his jaw, having a silent debate with his body to stay still. Athena always pushed the envelope. And obviously she was still up to her tricks. But he could resist. He had to resist. Damn it. He couldn't believe his eyes.

She stood waist deep and untied her bikini top. Then

balling it up in her hand, she tossed it and it landed on the edge. Then she bent over, her hands disappearing below the water surface, and righted herself with a matching piece to the discarded swimwear. This was tossed with more force, landing on the tip of his right shoe.

"Athena, you can't do this."

"Is it against the law? I've seen a few nude sunbathers on this island."

"No, it's not against the law," he said through gritted teeth. "Maybe I need to add skinny-dipping to the employee code of conduct, for your sake."

"Do you want me to come out?" She grinned as she walked forward. The waterline descended slowly past her belly button to her hips. She felt so uninhibited and free.

"Stop!" He was faced with her bared breasts or her fully nude body. Choices that made him blush.

"I'm getting cold. I'll have to go back in or come out and get a towel." She lowered her body, waving her arms below the water. "Come in. Join me. Look, we're consenting adults. I'll still let you boss me." She winked at him.

Collin growled. Words eluded him. The moment didn't call for his rational explanations because Athena wouldn't entertain his dissertation. She was more than a handful. And this tug-of-war with her always had him landing on her side of the line. No matter how hard he tried, he couldn't turn away from her. He didn't want to.

He wanted to kiss her, cup her breasts, feel her between his legs. He wanted so much.

He wanted her.

Now.

He pulled his shirt over his head and tossed it aside. What the hell was he doing? He pulled off his shoes and socks. At the water's edge, he stood with his hands on his hips, staring at Athena playing a water siren.

"I've made rules," Athena shouted at him.

"What rules?"

"I get to be the boss here. In this domain."

"Okay." Giving up control to Athena could be a dangerous move. But he wanted to be with her too much to care.

"Pants and briefs off."

He complied. She didn't have to grin with such enthusiasm. He hurried to the water and almost shot out at the shock of cold water.

"It'll be fine in a few seconds. It's better if you just jump in."

Collin waded out and sank down, waiting for his body to adjust to the new temperature. He watched Athena submerge and swim over to him, the air bubbles disclosing her approach. Her hands landed on his legs, sliding up, teasing him, dragging along his hips before she emerged from the water.

Without talking, thinking, waiting, he kissed her. He wrapped his arms around her, enjoying the softness of her breasts crushed against his chest. Heat rose between them, intense and searing. Her lips matched his in its quest to stir passion and emotion in each other. He plunged his tongue, only offering what she accepted.

She pressed against him, inciting a range of emotions that all stayed in the sensually hot category. Detaching from her mouth for air did nothing to tone down his emotions. He kissed her earlobe. His hands rubbed along the length of her back, sliding down to her hips.

"Let's head to the beach." She gasped. "Otherwise we may drown."

Collin hoisted her around his hips and made his way back to shore. Instead of the uneven shoreline, he headed for a lush covering for their comfort. He lowered her to the grassy carpet, taking a moment to enjoy the view of her body.

Athena didn't mind his bold examination. His admiration of her breasts hardened her nipples in anticipation. His scrutiny traveled the length of her body, lingering, visually stroking the spot between her legs. Every part of her warmed like a blushing maiden.

"You're beautiful all over."

"And I'd like to repay the compliment." She traced her hand along his pectoral muscles, moving from the smooth wide muscle in the chest to the dark nipple. He sucked in his breath when her thumb rubbed the sensitive nub.

His response to her teasing was to lower his head to her breast. His warm mouth covered her nipple, drawing it up with erotic pleasure. His tongue flicked over, making her teeth clench. She arched back, pushing her chest into the air. Her body ached for his touch. He could use his fingers, the palm of his hand or, her favorite, the touch of his tongue.

"What do you want from me?" Collin asked while his head rested on her chest.

"All that you have to offer…and then some."

"You turn my mind into mush."

"I'll take that as an accomplishment." She reached up to pull him on top of her body. "Why do you resist me?"

"Because you are a threat to my school." He stroked her nipple. "I'm putting the school in jeopardy by being with you."

"Trust me. I'll keep the secret." She crossed her heart.

"Don't do that, please." He closed his eyes as if in pain, except for the slight smile tugging his mouth.

"Do what?" She blew at his lips. "You mean crossing my heart." She retraced the spot, letting her finger linger and trail the outline of her areola. She had to bite down because teasing him also stirred up her juices.

She kissed his lips softly, running her hands over his buttocks. Her body ached for more than his lips. She encircled his hips with her legs, thrusting up her pelvis with an open invitation.

"You're a wicked woman."

"And you're a stubborn man."

"I'm a simple man who didn't have any worries. That is until I met you. You're a minx."

"Calling me names won't help your condition." She stroked him between his legs. His vice grip on her wrist halted the process.

"We can't do anything. I don't have protection. Who walks around with stuff?"

Athena pushed him off her. She walked over and retrieved her clothes, putting them on. After a few minutes, Collin followed suit, looking confused and more than a bit disappointed by the change of events.

"Let's go to your house to finish part two."

"Okay. And I'll get what we'll need to continue."

Only a cop restraining either one of them could have stopped their progress. Athena drove twenty miles above the speed limit grateful that many cars were off the road on a weekend. She didn't mind pausing in their hot action because as much as she liked the outdoor setting to get her groove on, she wasn't that much of an adventurer with the dense foliage as a backdrop and no protection.

After the dutiful stop at a local convenience store, Athena followed Collin to a beautiful house that she suspected was his home. She pulled up in the driveway behind him. Hopefully he hadn't gotten cold feet. She didn't want to be sent home unfulfilled.

"Welcome to my home." He opened her car door and offered his hand to help her exit the vehicle.

Athena stepped out and headed for the house. Once she entered the cool setting, she spun around to him. "Anyone home?"

"No. My housekeeper is off on the weekends."

"Good to know." She stripped out of her clothes and savagely pulled off his clothes. The drive to his home was an inconvenience, but it wasn't long enough to subdue her desire.

When Collin was fully undressed, he tossed her over his shoulder. With a hand firmly in place over her butt, he ran up the stairs and headed down the hallway. Athena couldn't stop giggling, playfully patting his backside.

He tossed her down in the middle of the bed, then tended to himself with the latex. She pushed herself up against the pillows. But his hands restrained her by the ankles. He slid her legs apart, still not letting go.

"I want to pleasure you."

She writhed in place, dying to feel his intimate touch. When he kissed a path on the inner side of her leg, she had to concentrate to stay cool. But she failed when her whimpers erupted from her. He continued up past her knee. She was sure that tears formed from the sheer pleasure. His lips blazed a trail, leading to that intimate place that couldn't wait to welcome him.

She grabbed the sheets in her tight fists, grinding her hips into the bed. He touched the intimate folds. Kissed and honored her in a way that she couldn't imagine. His hands continued to pin her legs and he slowly worked on her, laving her with his tongue. She almost cried as her body reacted with her personal essence.

Then he straddled her body. His eyes glazed with desire sucked her in with hypnotic power. She enjoyed the view of his body aroused and the epitome of male specimen. His body exuded the male physical and very sexual power. She practically drooled over his wide shoulders that tapered to his chiseled waist, to lean hips where his muscular thighs defined his long legs. Without his prompting, she placed her hand on his muscled chest. A part of her didn't think any of this was real. His arousal throbbed as her hand moved down his body. Its impatience was duly noted. And she liked teasing him as she worked his skin with small massage techniques. He twitched and she grinned that now she could be the dominant one to taunt him. But she had to work hard to resist his devilish grin that made her stomach do flip-flops.

"I want to touch you." She slid her hands down below his belly button. "You're beautiful."

"Close your eyes."

"No way." She wanted to hear him beg.

"Please."

"That's better."

"Focus on my voice."

"Okay." She licked her lips that needed moisture.

He placed a hand behind her back. "Relax," he whispered into her ear. "I will not hurt you. If you want me to stop, say the word. I want you, but I won't take you. Not yet."

He took her hand and placed it around his shaft that had swollen to a thickness that she found pleasing. Her hand surrounded the shaft and slid down to the tip where she caressed.

"Open your legs for me, please."

"Touch me." Athena didn't stop attending to him. She had to muster all her concentration to keep her legs from buckling when Collin's fingers slipped between her legs. He deftly stroked, circling the moist entrance.

"Athena, you bewitch me." He uttered her name like a hand gently stroking the contours of her face. The fine, deep timbre of his voice seduced her with its velvet quality.

"And you're robbing me of my sanity." She took his hand and guided him in how he should pleasure her.

He smiled, showing an even set of perfect white teeth. The man belonged among the gods of desire and virility, lording his power over female seduction. From here she noticed his thickly lashed eyes were the color of English toffee.

"How did I get so lucky to find you?" he asked.

"The power of the universe set both of us on the same path to meet and discover our sensual and sexual power."

He slipped his fingers deep inside her, while rubbing the external sensitive spot with his thumb. She ground her hips against his fingers that worked her like a refined jazz musician.

"You don't believe that it was just a fluke?"

She gasped as his fingers continued to work her. "No." And some credit had to go to the waterfall.

"I want you. I can't hold on." His voice hitched.

She wrapped her legs around his legs, offering herself to him. She wanted to be impaled, aching for him to fill her. Her nails dug into his butt cheeks.

Taking her cue, he slid into her. His body shook from the restraint. She appreciated his effort and set the pace for the ride.

"I want to be on top."

Without letting her go, he flipped their bodies. Athena settled on top of him ready to get her groove on. She rode him, sliding along his shaft, grinding her hips down in a rhythm that had cosmic relevance.

Holding on to his shoulders, rocking to their own beat raised her to another level of consciousness. All her senses came alive, reacting to the intense pleasure as they journeyed together to that peak. Pressure built, scrambling her power of speech. She tried to say something, anything. But she couldn't even hold a thought in her head.

She reared back and his hands massaged her breasts, adding more fuel to the fire that raged between her legs.

And then the explosions occurred, some small, but mostly large. Her climactic response pushed a guttural scream from deep within her.

Luckily Collin refused to let her go and joined her with an orgasm that rocked his entire body. His face contorted as if in pain. Athena leaned down and kissed his forehead to ease away the tightness. They stayed locked in each other's arms, allowing for a natural process as they wound down from the frenetic pace.

Collin looked down at Athena asleep on the other side of the bed. He couldn't sleep, although his body was exhausted from their marathon lovemaking. He eased off the bed and headed out to his veranda.

He sat in the lounge chair staring out into the darkness of his yard. No answer for the question paramount in his mind. What next?

"What next?" he whispered to the night. The line between work and personal bliss blurred almost into nonexistence. In there, a special woman had pushed aside the curtain, ushering in a wave of passionate possibilities. He'd given in like a weakling to satisfy his urges. Now reality didn't wait for sunrise. He rubbed his face, fighting against the regret. He didn't want to regret any ounce of it. What he shared with Athena was beautiful. Natural.

Dangerous.

Chapter 9

Athena didn't realize how difficult it was to keep her feelings secret for a few months. She sneaked away at every possible moment to be with Collin. Sometimes she thought the others may suspect something, but no one ever asked embarrassing questions or hinted. Too many times she canceled hanging out with Cicely.

Now, she took her place around the conference table. Their weekly staff meeting was due to begin. Finally Collin entered the room. She could tell that he hadn't slept well. His eyes had dark shadows beneath them. His clean-shaven face sported a shadow. His clothes were wrinkled.

He hadn't shared any bad news with her. But obviously something bothered him. She'd have to wait. In an attempt to avoid getting caught worrying over Collin, she adjusted her chair so that she could stare straight ahead. Casting him lingering looks like a high school girl with a crush couldn't happen.

"Good, everyone is here. Let's get started."

"We've lost several of the cleaning staff," Bill complained. "Looks like they got better-paying jobs on the big island."

"Some cleaning duties can be distributed among the students. It's their school. I think that it helps build pride if they have to take care of it," Athena said, remembering one such school in her childhood that got volunteers to pick up trash in the school yard. "The bigger, more complex jobs can go to a paid person."

"Sounds good to me." Cicely turned to Athena and offered a high five.

Collin nodded. "Okay, we'll give it a shot. Next item."

They ran through the various items on the agenda fairly quickly. Athena looked at her watch. Maybe she'd be able to sneak over to Collin's and enjoy the afternoon grilling steaks, relaxing and making love. She sighed.

"Athena, you have something to add?"

"Huh?" Athena looked at Lorraine. "No."

"Looked like you had your hand up."

"Nope." Athena moved her hand under the table.

"That's not quite true. Athena had mentioned the possibility of a field trip to coincide with the history, biology and math classes. Remember, you told me about it."

Athena remembered the conversation. But it wasn't in Collin's office or in her classroom. That conversation had occurred while she was lying naked next to him on the veranda as they gazed at the stars. Her face warmed from the memory.

"We've never had a field trip because of the liability," Lorraine explained. "Has something changed? I think it's a fantastic idea."

"We are covered. I think we should give it a shot. Let's look at the lesson plans and see how we can integrate the trips to make it worthwhile." Collin looked pleased.

"I'd be happy to help with the logistics. Anyone care to work with me?" Athena volunteered.

"I'll help you." Cicely raised her pencil. "Lorraine? Thelma?"

"I don't think you need all of us to plan it. Come up with something that we can work with and present it," Lorraine replied.

Athena didn't know what exactly was wrong, but she detected a frosty edge at times from Lorraine. Maybe she was mistaken because they had no misgivings between them. And when she looked at Lorraine, as she did now, the woman smiled back at her. Yet she didn't feel as if there was any warmth and it certainly didn't involve any part of her face.

"If there's nothing else, I'll end the meeting," Collin stated.

"I think we're done," Thelma said, looking around for the room.

Everyone scattered. There had been a time when they would plan what they would do together. Lately everyone had their own plans. Lorraine had taken up nature walks. Thelma and Bill were always at the movies. Cicely had calmed down with the nightlife. Now she was always sitting at the dining-room table crafting games, puzzles and other activities for the younger kids.

Athena looked up at Collin. She wanted him. Hopefully he could read her silent message from across the room.

His wink said it all.

Athena wanted to rip off his shirt right there. But Lorraine's slight cough at the side of the room put on the brakes. Seeing that Lorraine wasn't getting up, Athena picked up her notepad and pen. She pushed in the chair, hoping that her coworker would do the same. She didn't budge. Feeling guilty about skipping out on preparing dinner, Athena turned down any secret plans to meet Collin.

Later that evening, Athena helped prepare the dinner. Thelma and Cicely were in good spirits, chatting about the fresh vegetables that had come from the garden. Athena never embraced the garden patch in the backyard. But she didn't mind congratulating them on their success.

When the pasta was at a full boil, the front door opened. Lorraine came in and slammed it shut. Everyone in the kitchen looked up. She didn't look at any of them as she stormed into her room.

"She's been in a rotten mood lately." Cicely chewed on a string bean. "I think it must be personal stuff. She's been writing a lot of letters."

"She never talks about her family." Thelma picked up her own string bean to chew.

"I'll go see what's up." Athena didn't really want to be the one to chat with Lorraine, but they all lived in the house. It was too small quarters for any one of them to be upset.

She knocked on the door. For the length of her stay, she had been in Lorraine's room only twice. The woman was intensely private, very loyal and had a strong work ethic. Next to her, Athena usually felt as if she wasn't doing enough or wasn't working hard enough.

"Come in."

"Hey, you looked upset?" Athena closed the door behind her but stayed near it, waiting for her invitation to sit.

"It's been a rough week. I think that I'm coming down with the flu."

"I've had a couple girls in my class with some type of a bug. I hope that I don't get it." She chuckled but it sounded forced.

"What do you want?"

Lorraine's bluntness stunned her to momentary silence.

"Didn't mean to sound rude. I really am not feeling good. I'll lie down and take it easy for the rest of the day."

"I'll let Thelma and Cicely know. You've been running yourself ragged. We're all here to help you, just tell us what to do." Athena reached for her arm, but Lorraine pulled away.

Athena's hand paused and then she dropped her hand to the side. If she had the courage, she'd press Lorraine for an answer, a reason why she didn't want to be around her. This wasn't her imagination. She'd done something wrong, but couldn't understand what had offended Lorraine.

"I'll go." Athena walked out of the room, still a little shaken.

"How is she?" Cicely came up to her. Athena held up a hand, restraining her enthusiasm. "She wants to be left alone. Needs to rest this evening."

"What about dinner?" Thelma asked. She opened the pot of pasta and moved it to another burner. "Our dinner will be ruined."

"No, it won't. Move over, I'll help. We'll have our traditional Saturday dinner and it will be fabulous." Athena bumped Thelma's shoulder playfully, grabbing her string bean.

She glanced at Lorraine's closed bedroom door. At times like this when she was home, if her sorority sisters had any issues with each other, one of them would take the role to squash it.

The four of them may not be sorority sisters, but they had the same alliance and need to get along. And these women had become more than coworkers. They had become friends. Reconciling with Lorraine would come at some point.

Dinner was mostly quiet with small peppering of conversation. They all looked up at Lorraine's door when she came out, but she didn't look at them. Instead she went out the front door and never returned.

"I don't like this," Cicely complained. "This is so not like her."

"We all have our off days," Thelma offered.

They finished the meal. Tension hung heavily, adding a stifling layer of discomfort over them. But Athena refused to let it seep into her thoughts. In her world, everything was going fine.

"Ladies, I'll head out shortly." Now she could head

to Collin's without feeling guilty that she hadn't spent time with her roommates.

"Don't stay out too late. Collin was all over us the last time you did that."

"He's quite the worrywart."

"That's because you're his favorite," Cicely teased.

"Stop that. I recall that he was all over himself when you were in your altercation."

"That's right. He got that guy kicked the heck off the island. Now that's what I wanted as a big brother in high school." Thelma grinned.

They all laughed, remembering what hellish experiences they suffered in high school or maybe even college. The remainder of the afternoon they spent on the porch sipping on wine spritzers talking about their high school crushes and the toads who turned into handsome princes. As the sun dipped, Athena didn't regret not heading off to Collin's right away. They had spent quality time rebuilding their camaraderie.

"I missed not having you stay over last night." Collin kissed the side of Athena's neck, enjoying hearing her small giggle.

"We're having a crisis at the house. Lorraine is in a nasty mood."

"You're telling me. She snapped my head off. I backed off. But her lesson plans have been slipping. Not that I'm the type to stick to rules." His hand slipped around her waist. "But I wanted to see how she was going to work the math with the field trip."

"It's been like that for at least two weeks. And I'm not her favorite person."

"Maybe it's family." Collin slipped his hand under her blouse and cupped her breast.

"We thought about that." Athena's breathing grew faster. "I'm not so sure."

"Can you help her with the field trip project? I'd like to do the field trip in at least one day but no more than three days." He slid her breast out of the bra and played with her nipple. She pushed her hips against him, stirring him up in similar fashion. He pulled her hair off her neck where he delivered kisses along the length of her neck.

She leaned her head back against his shoulder and sighed.

"I could hold you like this all day."

"I know, but it will make teaching my class very difficult." She slid away from him, straightening her clothes. "What if someone walked into your office?"

"I've locked it."

Athena rushed over to the door. "You can't do that. It makes it more suspicious."

Collin shrugged. "Doesn't bother me."

She unlocked the door and opened it slightly. "I'm heading back to class, you crazy man."

A knock on the door startled them.

"Come in." He wasn't expecting anyone. Then Lorraine came into view. She glared at him as she approached with papers in hand.

He looked down at the papers, wondering what she was delivering.

"I'll leave you now." Athena stepped out from the

corner. He hadn't noticed that she'd melted in the dark area of his office. Even Lorraine jumped at the sound of her voice. Neither woman looked at each other as Athena rushed out the office.

"I've brought the plan for the field trip."

"Oh. Thank you. I was just talking about this to Athena."

"Really, why?"

"I thought maybe you needed help."

"I didn't ask for any help. And I'm quite capable of asking for what I need. Haven't I always done that?"

He stood to offer reassurance. She took a step back but thrust the papers at his chest. He caught the stapled pack, holding fast to her wrist.

"Lorraine, what is the problem? You're falling apart and everyone is worried."

"And that's what Athena was complaining about in here?"

"I'm not going to address that because your tone is inappropriate. Have a seat, let me go through this."

Lorraine stuffed her hands in her back pocket, staring at him. He didn't want to engage in a staring contest and broke contact before resuming his seat behind the desk.

"I got one of the hotels to donate lunches to the children."

She nodded.

"We will have to rent a few more vans."

"I can take care of that."

He refrained from saying that Athena would do that task. Instead he allowed her to take it on. It meant that he'd talk to Athena about the change. Having Lorraine step up was what he'd come to expect from her and he was glad that she was willing.

"All right, I'll get back to work."

"Thanks for this." He raised the papers in his hand.

She smiled and he wondered if he was just making a big deal out of nothing. Maybe she was simply having a bad couple of days. As she closed the door, he sighed. His school was important, but his staff wasn't far behind. They were all in this together.

A week later they headed out on the first day of the field trip. The first stop was Fort Franklin, where the British took dominance of the island from the Spanish. Then they'd headed to the Banes Plantation, where the sugar cane plantation in the early 1800s thrived on slave labor. Finally they'd stopped in at the only American hotel that would provide lunch and access to the beach for their students.

Athena looked forward to the day. She drove one van, introducing the children to songs that she and Asia had sung with her parents on many road trips. Their voices rose in chorus, a few out of tune, but managed to catch on to the easy rhyming lyrics.

"Everyone ready to have fun?" Athena called over her shoulder.

"Yes, Miss Athena," they responded.

Athena laughed and sped up to catch the van in front of her. They traveled along to one of the highest points of the island, ideal for military defense. Fort Franklin was named after the Admiral Dover Franklin, who landed on the island several years before the final altercation with the Spanish. The island's history had been domination of one empire or another. Now the three cultures of French, Spanish and English lived on the small land in separate territories, but for the most part peaceful. The fort was partially destroyed from the salt in the air. But there was still a major portion that remained intact.

Athena stood at the lookout point with a good view of the Atlantic Ocean. Its emerald-green color had gemlike quality.

"Make sure you listen to the tour guide, everyone. There will be a test next week."

A collective groan could be heard. Athena laughed, remembering her school trips and teachers' similar threats or promises to hand out a test. She had an assignment in mind, but it wasn't a test. She simply wanted them to practice their creative writing skills.

The visit to the plantation ended as a quick trip with the skies overcast. The staff was nervous with the impending storm and didn't want to take chances, moving up their sightseeing list. By the time the skies broke and torrential rain occurred, they were in a hotel enjoying a sizable lunch.

"Maybe when we retire, we can enjoy the leisurely life and tour all the islands." Cicely sat back munching on pieces of papaya.

"Let me know when you buy the tickets. I may have to hook my trailer to your Maserati," Athena joked.

"I'll be a boy toy for some rich widow." Bill joined in their conversation and earned a few groans for his contribution.

"Hey, who is that?" Thelma sat up, craning her neck.

"Who are you talking about?" Athena followed her line of vision, but didn't see anything out of the ordinary.

"Who is the man talking to Collin? He looks important." Thelma held Athena's chin, guiding her to where she was talking about.

"That's the kingpin Thadeus Kitchner." Lorraine didn't bother to hide behind anything. She leaned over the balcony, staring down at the men in an intense conversation.

Athena joined her, noting the security detail that hovered in easy reach. She looked at Collin, wondering why he was talking to this man. His arms were animated as he continually banged one hand into the palm of the other hand. Whatever the conversation, Collin wasn't happy.

"Looks like Kitchner is conducting business."

"I can't see Collin working with a drug kingpin."

"Oh, Kitchner is into more than drugs. Prostitution. Government corruption. He is quite a multitasker."

"I'm going down there." Athena turned to leave.

"No, you're not." Lorraine grabbed her by the arm. "You don't want to be in his crosshairs. I'm sure Collin doesn't need our help."

Athena didn't budge and with Lorraine's grip on her arm, she couldn't move even if she wanted to. She'd find out from Collin later why he was talking to such a bad character. Hopefully she could accept his answer, whatever it was.

Before they could duck out of sight, Kitchner pointed in their direction. Collin looked up at them. Athena didn't mistake his fury, although he showed great restraint.

Lorraine sniffed. "Let's hope he didn't sell his soul to the devil."

Chapter 10

After all the planning and coordinating, Collin couldn't say that he remembered how the field trip wrapped up. Kitchner making a surprise visit to ensure face time with him had the effect of exploding any sense of euphoria. Every point the man made added notches to raise Collin's anger. He recalled ending the conversation with lots of gesticulating and definitive statements colorfully decorated with intermittent curses. Kitchner tried to calm him, but stopped when he realized anything that he said compounded the situation. A day later he couldn't shake the unsettled feeling.

"Why don't you tell me what happened yesterday?" Athena rolled over and scooted her body closer to him.

"Because it was nothing special. Business. And, no, not school business."

"You're being evasive. Although I am curious, I'm not prying into your affairs."

"Don't get yourself worked up." He pulled her closer to his body and kissed her forehead.

"Should I be worried about this Kitchner?" She rubbed his chest. "Or should I be worried about you?"

"How do you know his name?"

"According to my sources, the whole island knows his name." She paused. "But what puzzles me is why people make innuendos about him and you."

Collin hadn't wanted to think about his relationship with Athena. He didn't want to think about where it would lead. Probing questions full of nasty potential could take things between them a bit too far. How much should he open his heart to her? The trouble was he couldn't answer definitively.

Athena positioned herself onto her stomach and propped her chin. She locked gazes with him. "You can trust me." Athena kissed him on his chest.

He'd start with revealing just the basics. "Kitchner delves in illegal business on the island and other islands. I took this property, but nothing else."

She sucked in her breath.

"I know, you don't have to issue the warning. But I was desperate. He offered the building and I took it."

"You paid nothing?"

"I paid, but nothing like what it would be worth on the open market. I also asked him to leave my staff alone and definitely leave the students alone."

"So…what does he want now?" She slid her body upward to his face, where she rested her forehead against his chin.

"He's warning me. Nothing in particular." He didn't dare tell her that Kitchner's competitors were threatened by the school. They accused him of affecting their recruiting efforts. Single mothers weren't as likely to hand over their girls because the girls now had options. The young boys weren't immune, either.

He'd have to pay another visit to the commissioner.

"You did get rid of him, right?"

"I'd like to think so." All he'd done was poke at the rattlesnake. Kitchner and his kind had enough venom to make him stay clear.

"You're my warrior hero."

"I'll take the warrior part. The hero suit doesn't quite fit."

Athena touched his chin with her finger. "You are either crazy or brave." She leaned up and kissed his mouth.

Collin closed his eyes and blew out any further thought of Kitchner. The situation had been moved to the back of his mind. The man accused him of delaying the inevitable. But he didn't want to dwell on the past or be preoccupied with the future. The present contained Athena in his arms and that was all that mattered.

He gathered her in his arms and slipped her under him. She smelled faintly of vanilla, a scent that he came to associate with her. He inhaled deeply, wishing he could erase the ugliness. She held him with a gentleness that nudged at his heart.

"You mean so much to me," he admitted. He kissed

her, softly and gently, waking up her mouth with languid strokes. His fingers slid into her thick, silky hair.

Whenever he held her close, he lost himself in her essence.

"Baby, I can't get enough of you." This time when he kissed her, he caressed her skin that was soft and smooth. "You're like a chocolate sundae."

"That sounds yummy." She groaned.

He kissed her neck, blazing a path to the familiar indentation at the base of her neck. When she arched her neck, pushing up her breasts, he acted upon the offer. Each brown tip earned his attention, as he sucked them to a tight bud.

Her hands played with his hair, massaging his temples with a sensual touch. It was his turn to groan with pleasure, pure and unadulterated. He rubbed his cheek against the fullness of her breast, lingering over the continued scent of vanilla. He almost envied her daily ritual of lotioning her body. That was a treat he would have preferred to do.

But he didn't mind reenacting his fantasy because he had a bottle of massage oil. He popped open the bottle and poured a little in the palm of his hand. Slowly he rubbed his hands together, grinning at her enthusiasm.

Her eyes closed as she licked her lips. Her moistened lips tantalized him, slightly open, teasing, inviting. Just looking at her turned him on.

She took his hands and placed them on her shoulders, moving his hands down over her breasts, not fast, but slow, allowing him to feel every twitch of muscle under her skin. Every nuance about her he looked forward to learning. Massaging the oil around her breasts, along her sides, over her stomach, under her belly button down to the delicate triangle between her legs.

Her legs twitched as he paused before planting a kiss. Each leg he administered more oil from her thigh down to her polished toes. Even her giggle excited him as his finger grazed her instep.

"You know I'm not done with you."

"I can't stand it anymore. I want you," she wailed.

"I could do what you say, but I'm not ready to obey." He turned her over. "It's my turn to play the boss."

"But you are the boss. That's not really role-playing."

"And since when have you treated me as the boss? From the time your feet stepped onto the tarmac on this island, you've been nudging me, sitting on me and, at times, outright kicking me out of the driver's seat." He poured the oil directly on her back in the valley of her spine. Her body jerked, but he held her down. "Nope, I think punishment is due."

He spread the oil along her back, rubbing from her neck out to her shoulders. She moaned. The sound vibrated through her chest under him.

"Don't get comfortable." He kissed her neck. "I'm expecting a heck of a tip for my services."

"I want you to know that I have a long memory."

He rubbed the oil down to the base of her behind, taut and darn beautiful. The sheen of the oil accentuated her lean physique. Again he admired her to the point where his thoughts turned into a ramble. His desire was plain and simple.

Duped by her sudden quiet form, he was caught off guard when she suddenly turned under him.

"Your boss persona has expired." She held him intimately, stroking him into a blithering idiot.

"Stop," he hissed. He grabbed her wrists, needing a moment to calm himself, to get back equilibrium.

"Then give it to me."

He growled. Groaning wasn't working on her.

From her small chuckle, growling didn't work either.

She raised her hips, sending him a private invitation. He accepted, promptly sliding into her. And once they were united, he set the rhythm.

They moved together, as one, fully engaged in the warm blanket of rapture. Pressure expanded. Their energy built. Together they took the express to the top, pushing harder to take them higher and higher, cresting to the ultimate peak. And when the explosion occurred, he gripped her shoulders and buried his head against her cheek, praying he could keep from howling.

She wrapped him in her embrace until the end.

Later that week bored out of her mind, Athena was at the women's house listening to the weather report. Collin had been out of touch and she had to keep herself busy. She grew worried about the intensity of the storm. Nothing sounded positive, even with the vagueness of the various scenarios. The worst part of what she felt was that she didn't know how to prepare. The cupboards were stocked. She'd seen enough movies and documentaries to know about the extensive damage of wind and rain. After braving through so many challenges, she didn't want to be outdone by a tropical storm.

"Every year since the school started, the summer tropical storms have pounded us. Twice we missed the hurricane-force winds because they blew past the island," Lorraine explained at the commercial break.

"Last year was pretty wicked. But we had enough time to prepare. That seems to make the difference in how much damage we sustain." Thelma pulled out several flashlights from a brown paper bag. She'd recently done some shopping.

"How much time do we have?" Athena asked, shifting her attention from Thelma to Lorraine, whose mood seemed improved.

"If it blows past the island as everyone is hoping, then we'll only get the heavy rains in about two days." Lorraine looked at all of them, then continued. "But if it changes paths, then we may not get a lot of time."

"What about the kids?" Athena thought about all her girls. She had driven Marigold home this evening. Maybe she should've kept her at the house.

"Most times they'll start evacuating. Some people go. Unfortunately many stay to protect their belongings."

"Can we bring the kids here?" Athena wanted to do something productive.

"We aren't equipped to be a haven. It's a risk."

"Forget about the risk. We've got solid walls. This place is built like a fortress." Athena jumped up, her adrenaline racing. She didn't care if she sounded screwy. "I'm going to get as many girls as possible."

"And what if they have siblings? What about the parents? What about grandparents? Are you really going to be responsible for taking care of several panicked girls?" Lorraine stopped talking, rubbing her forehead with such ferocity that she left a red imprint. "The policy is that if people come here, we won't turn them away. But we can't go get them."

Athena heard Lorraine's explanation, but couldn't accept what she said. There was no way that she could sit here, relatively safe, while her girls could be in danger in their homes that couldn't withstand a stiff breeze.

Frustrated, she retorted, "I'm going for a walk." She shrugged off their protests and headed outside.

Quick footsteps approached. Cicely appeared at her side. They walked silently toward the beach. The air felt heavy and expectant. Stillness hung in suspended animation around them. The trees didn't sway. The birds didn't chirp. Only the loud crunching sound of their feet against the rocky shore broke the silence.

Athena paused to look out toward the ocean. She tried to imagine what the fury of the Atlantic would look like. The gentle rolling waves carried by currents didn't appear dangerous. She stepped closer, inhaling the salty air. She didn't feel impervious to the danger, but she also wasn't going to hide and wait.

"I'm going to get as many girls as I can," she restated her stance.

"But what about what Lorraine said? She does make sense." Cicely's worry came through loud and clear.

"Will you help me?"

"Don't be stubborn. This isn't about you versus Lorraine. I've noticed that you and her have been going at it."

"Stop the madness. Why would I have anything against Lorraine?" Athena frowned, feeling uncomfortable that someone else confirmed her feeling. However, Cicely was wrong. She wasn't trying to battle with Lorraine.

Cicely kept pace with her. "You've come in and taken over. The men listen to you. They look forward to talking to you at dinner. When you're not there, the conversation is dead around the table. The students, even the ones not in your class, talk about you. All of that used to be Lorraine. She is like the blond bomber. And you came in full of all-American-girl energy and looks." Cicely looked down, kicking at the little rocks littering the beach. "Then there is Collin."

"What about Collin?" Athena stopped. She couldn't concentrate on the conversation *and* walk.

"He used to come to Lorraine for advice and had her lead the projects. He relied on her."

"But I don't have anything to do with that." Athena's face warmed with the direction of this conversation.

"That may be true, but you just need to be sensitive. Give Lorraine her space."

Athena walked a few feet to process what Cicely was telling her. She didn't want to come in creating chaos among the group. But she also refused to back down. She'd come on the job with the intention of doing something meaningful. Facing challenges, not being a coward. Her grandmother had taken on school boards and administrations. She'd done what felt right in her heart.

"Cicely, don't take this the wrong way, but if I can get

Collin to approve what I'm doing, then I will do it."
Abruptly she turned around and headed back to the
house.

Athena drove over to Collin's house, hoping that he
was there. She didn't want to call and make her request.
Considering that her idea was going over like a lead
balloon, she'd rather appeal to him in person. When she
pulled up, there were cars parked in the driveway.

She debated on whether to continue with her visit.
With company, she may not get his undivided attention.
Her idea was too important and time-sensitive not to be
properly addressed.

Lynette, his housekeeper, opened the door the moment
Athena's foot hit the first step leading up to the porch.

"Athena, Mr. Winslow is occupied at the moment."

Athena stopped short. She was momentarily confused by Lynette's new guard duty. Her face didn't show
that she was kidding.

"I want to tell him something of an important nature.
It's about the hurricane," she clarified, sensing that
being vague wasn't going to win over the housekeeper.

"Please wait in the study."

Athena knew where the study was located, yet she
couldn't edge past the housekeeper, who led the way
with deliberate steps. She heard voices, but couldn't
see anyone. Darting into one of the rooms off to the side
did cross her mind.

"I'll get Mr. Winslow. Please have a seat."

Athena tried the door after the housekeeper left.
The door opened, but Lynette was standing on the
other side, as if expecting her to try an escape. With a

disgusted huff, the housekeeper walked away. Athena, embarrassed, closed the door and retreated into the room.

She sat on the edge of the heavy desk, hoping that Collin wouldn't be long. Maybe on the way out, she'd get a chance to see who had come visiting.

And it better not be a woman.

"Athena, what are you doing here?"

Now that wasn't the reception she expected. She waited for him to start laughing and tease her shocked expression. As he got closer, she recognized that he wasn't playing. She'd come to know the signs when he slid a barrier to keep anyone, including her, out of his business. She played the cavalier role well, pretending that she was too independent to care. Experiencing the hurt from his rejection underscored that lie.

"I'm in the middle of an important meeting. Can this wait?"

"I wanted to know if I have permission to get the girls to shelter with us at the school."

"What? Why?"

"The tropical storm is coming through and I figured because we had the space and stronger house that we could help our students."

He nodded, taking in her explanation. But he didn't look as if he had been persuaded. Several times he looked over his shoulder, as if preoccupied with the other business, much to her irritation.

"Sorry if what I'm saying isn't important."

"Calm down." He motioned with his hands to keep

it down. "Lorraine called me to say that you'd jumped off the plank by yourself to play hero."

"Was that a quote?"

"If you can get everyone to help you, then fine. And I mean everyone. I don't want any of that superhero crap going on. People's lives are at stake."

"Fine." Athena didn't expect this chilly reception and condescending counseling session. She brushed past him.

He grabbed her arm and pulled her to him. They stood with bodies pressed against each other. Tension crackled between them.

She knew that he wanted her to kiss him. Hell, she wanted to kiss him. But his message and tone proved that he didn't really get her point. This effort was bigger than all of them. There were lives at stake.

"Don't be angry, baby." He kissed her forehead and raised her chin with the crook of his finger.

"I'm not," she lied.

"Good. I have to get back to my meeting. Here, take my van. It's bigger and has more space. You'd better get under way. You might not have an hour before the storm breaks."

She grabbed the keys deliberately holding on to his hand. With or without anger, her skin tingled from the contact. She wanted him to acknowledge what they naturally created between them. He couldn't simply set the elusive feeling aside.

"Shall I return the keys tonight?" She allowed the question to hover suggestively.

He hesitated.

A cold splash of fear gripped her. Was she an item

that had worn out its welcome? She needed the keys; otherwise she'd have thrown it at him.

"I'll come over to the house later to see how everyone is doing."

Of course he'd check on the children.

"Thanks." She walked out into the hallway, expecting to be escorted out. Instead she made it to the front door alone. The muffled voices that she'd heard were now silent. Had he told his guest to remain silent and out of sight?

Outside she noticed that the cars were still there. Who exactly was visiting Collin? She headed down the steps, but instead of going to the other van, she walked along the side of the house. On this side of the house, she should have a clear view of the living room and dining area that opened onto a covered balcony in the back.

She stopped and eased closer to the house. Several heads, all males, were sitting and smoking in the back. She saw Collin reappear and take a seat among the men. They were all slapping him on his back and they shared a laugh.

But the humor was lost on her. To see him smiling and joking with these various men, one of whom was Kingpin Kitchner, made her sick to the stomach. What he had told her before they made love and what she was seeing now didn't connect.

"What is going on?" she muttered.

Did he need money? Was the school part of a money-laundering or drug-running scheme?

She gritted her teeth, fighting back the urge to step

into view. All her talk about being courageous was sorely being tested. As she backed away and headed to the van, she hung her head that she'd failed on this count.

While she drove back to the house, her thoughts were her only companion. She pulled up and parked, wishing she could be alone for a bit. No matter what she saw, she couldn't completely believe that Collin had stepped to the dark side.

Chapter 11

"What happened? I see you got the van." Cicely leaned against the driver's door. Her eyes were bright with her admiration. "You are the woman!" She chuckled. "You know Lorraine is going to be a little green."

Athena listened to Cicely's chatter, hiding her own pain from view. She went through the motions of high-fiving and hugging Cicely. Many times she wished that Cicely had access to joining her sorority, Xi Theta Sigma. Her sincerity and desire to help children earned her a place in the organization.

They entered the house.

"Hey, ladies, guess what? Athena has the keys to the bigger van." She held up the keys, jingling them to the point of annoyance.

"And how does that affect me?" Lorraine asked as she pointedly looked at Athena.

"I need your help. I need everyone's help. Collin is okay with helping as many students as possible. It's up to the parents, though. And when we get full, then we're full."

"Count me out of this nonsense." Lorraine held up her hands and walked away.

"I can't do this unless everyone agrees. That's the deal."

Lorraine headed into the kitchen and helped herself to a soda. She didn't say anything as she gulped down the drink. No one spoke, switching their gazes from Lorraine back to Athena.

Athena maintained her reserve, trying not to react. They were wasting precious minutes over a battle of egos. If they were going to get moving, she'd have to take the big step.

"Lorraine, I know you think that I'm doing this only for my own glory. Maybe three months ago when I got here, I may have had that agenda. I wanted an experience that could define me or my worth. In that time, I've grown up. I've learned to be humble. I've learned to love these girls who are eager to learn, excelling in their classes and who now have a future that is open to them. Helping them during this storm is not about playing the hero. It's about doing what is right." She took a deep breath. "Will you please help me?"

She didn't have to look at Thelma and Cicely to know that they were in shock. She could see from her side view that their mouths were open. More important she kept her focus on Lorraine. Gaining her trust was paramount to their future relationship.

"I'll help." Lorraine set down the empty soda can and took a seat at the dining table. "Go ahead and get everyone together so we can discuss the game plan."

Athena wanted to celebrate Lorraine's understanding of her message. Not only was she willing to help, but she also didn't push her out of the way to take over.

An hour later, they had all the extra cots, sleeping bags and other supplies in the two houses. They had created makeshift beds in the classrooms, too. The kitchens had been recently stocked and could last for at least a week. If necessary, the adults would cut back their portions to extend the food supply.

Excitement buzzed like an electric current as everyone followed through on their tasks. Athena drove Collin's van so that Lorraine could drive the van she'd left. Now they had all three vans heading off to various areas of the islands. For many of the children, their families didn't have a phone. The staff would take their chances to go directly to the house and talk to the parents.

Athena created the order of her student pickup, hoping to eliminate having to double back. The first two families declined their offer because they had infants or toddlers and the girls were a helping hand. She could understand their position but was disappointed, nevertheless.

"We have Lucy next on our list." Cicely placed a check mark next to her name.

"Does Lucy have siblings?" Athena asked because they had the room with no one being rescued as yet.

"She's got a brother in Bill's class."

"Does that mean Bill is coming to the house?"

"We didn't talk about that." Cicely shrugged.

Athena didn't want to waste time, but didn't want to take the chance that Lucy got missed. She turned down the dirt road that would take her to the other side of the island.

As the van squeaked and rattled in protest of the potholes, clouds thick and dark rolled in as if pushed by an unseen hand. The wind picked up, casting a shrill whistle through the windows. Tree branches whipped into a frenzy. Debris from litter around the area swirled and then caught in the air current before slamming into impeding objects. The van served as a shield as they drove into the storm's fury.

Athena could barely make out the numbers on the houses, which only a few had. She'd never been to Lucy's house and didn't know where to go. People were nowhere in sight, although she saw dim lights in some windows. She offered a silent prayer on all their behalf.

"I think this is it on the right." Cicely hopped out of the van before she had come to a complete stop. The sudden change in the weather clearly rattled her. The bubbly, lighthearted attitude was nowhere in sight.

Athena didn't kill the engine. Every second counted. As she looked up through the windshield, she suspected the rainfall would come at any minute.

She joined Cicely at the door. They knocked, or more like banged, on the door.

"No one is home," Cicely yelled.

The wind keened like a sad dog howling. If they weren't on a mission, Athena would have gladly stayed at the house and hunkered down until the storm was over.

Athena took her turn pounding on the door. The result hadn't changed. No one answered.

"Well, either Bill got them or they took off to safe ground," Athena yelled to Cicely. "We can't wait any longer. One more stop. Marigold's." She hurried down the steps and back into the van.

The wind hadn't let up. And now fat raindrops plopped onto the van. The hazards of driving on the narrow road with blind corners and no traffic signs were dangerous. Now that precipitation and gusting winds were variables, the level of danger had reached extreme. Unfortunately they headed to the side of the island that would be hit first by the hurricane and was the farthest point out.

Athena gripped the steering wheel as if it was an anchor that could keep her steady. The van swayed from the wind gusts. She had encountered nasty weather living in Chicago, mainly blizzards and extreme frigid temperatures. Hurricanes weren't the norm.

And from her quick glances over at Cicely, Athena didn't have much support from the young woman who seemed to have lost inches in height. She had slid down the seat as if she could duck out of the path of the hurricane.

Lightning struck in jagged bright shafts of light. They lit a path in the darkened sky, finding their way to earth. The thunder popped as if a Roman god clapped his hands in the universe. Throughout the ride, this weather pattern played havoc with them.

Finally they reached Marigold's house. The downpour flooded the roads in minutes. They had to wade through murky water to get to the door. And from the rate of rising, the house would be underwater in a matter of minutes. By how much was the question.

"Miss Athena, you're here." Marigold rushed out of the house, clearly breaking free from her mother's grasp. She hugged Athena and then turned to Cicely for a quick hug. "I was getting scared."

Athena nodded, making sure to pay her greetings to Marigold's mother. "We came to offer the school as a refuge."

"For both of us?" Hope hung on the mother's words with quiet desperation.

"I'm sorry—" Cicely started.

Athena touched Cicely's shoulder. "Yes, we can take both of you. Get whatever you need, but I'll need you to make haste."

When they disappeared deeper into the house, gathering their belongings, Athena turned to Cicely. "Sorry, didn't mean to jump in there, but we've got an empty van. How could we justify leaving them?"

Cicely nodded.

An especially loud crack of thunder snapped their attention back to the matter at hand.

"Ladies, I need you to hurry."

"Here we come," Luisa called out. "Marigold, forget all of those books. We need to be able to move quickly."

Athena saw the distress and understood that Marigold wanted to hang on to items that could bring her comfort.

"How about three books? I don't think you'll have much time for anything else. I'll need you to assist me with the younger children."

Marigold smiled, willing to leave her precious books for the chance to work with her.

They headed out a few minutes later. The world had undergone a change. Pieces of wood from houses or barns flew light as feather through the air. A couple of times they had to step back into the house. Between the debris and the blowing rain, they contended with the possibility of being knocked unconscious or driving blindly.

A horrendous cracking sound erupted. The ground shook.

"Run!"

The side of the mountain broke loose, tumbling, sliding, crashing from one level to the next into a muddy avalanche.

"In the van!" Athena jumped in and cursed. She'd not only turned off the engine, but taken out the key. Now she had to dig it out of her pocket, wasting precious minutes.

The mud slide continued, picking up speed. Young trees, grasslands, the rocky face of the landscape didn't stand a chance. Everything was covered. And Marigold's home stood in its path. And after her home, they were next.

"Drive! Drive!" Cicily urged.

"Oh, no, Mommy." Marigold covered her eyes.

"Athena, start the damn car!" Luisa shouted, banging on the backseat of the car.

Athena bit down. She wanted to scream at everyone to shut up. She wanted to bang the steering wheel in frustration. And she wanted to cry because the engine wouldn't turn over.

   She tried again. This time she did cry. Not sobbing.
Not loud. Quiet. With long tears streaming down her
face. She couldn't bear to look into the rearview mirror
where Marigold and her mother sat huddled together.

   "It's not working," Athena stated. "We need to get out
of here." She wiped her eyes against her sleeve. "Let's
move it. Marigold, take only what you can carry in your
hands. We're going to have to haul it. Luisa, can you run?"

   "Watch me."

   The sound of the mud slide hitting the house was horrendous. In a few seconds, their home and possessions
were covered in mud. By the time the house completely
collapsed they were at the side road running for their lives.

   Collin had planned to go with the staff on their rescue
mission. But his impromptu guests didn't provide him
with the chance. Life certainly was getting complicated.
Everyone wanted something from him. He tried to
compromise. But certain things had no room for nego-
tiation.

   At least focusing on the weather prevented him from
dwelling on how far he had gone down a path that could
lead to trouble. In the classroom building, he surveyed
the sleeping areas. He was proud of Athena leading the
group to making this effort work. Now that she had im-
plemented the plan, he looked forward to being with the
children. They would be safe there and get all the attention that was necessary.

   A van pulled in and he immediately headed into the
rain. An umbrella was a joke in the windy, wet violence.
As the wind pushed against his body, he leaned in and

fought his way to the van. He had a pattern of one step forward, two steps back.

Finally he got to the door. Lorraine jumped out, shouting at him, but her words were lost. He opened the side passenger doors. Scared young faces stared back at him.

"Hey, everyone, I'm glad to see you. I'll need you to come out, one at a time, with one of us. Okay?"

They barely nodded. Every sound of the storm made them jump. He couldn't blame them.

Thelma and Lorraine joined him at the van's door. He quickly shared what they needed to do. At this point there was no game plan. It was each person's discretion that had to be their guide. What they did agree on doing was to get the children who looked like they couldn't hold it together into the classroom first. One panicked child could send the others into a frenzy and then they would resist rather than work with them.

As a loose bucket sailed through the air like a missile past his head, Collin didn't need any wild card from nature to affect this situation. They staggered how they retrieved the kids so no one was left unattended.

By the time he took the last child, his feet were ankle deep in mud. His clothes had become a second skin. And he could barely see more than a few inches in front of him as the rainfall acted like cotton gauze over his eyes.

Once they were all in the classroom, the door tightly shut and windows covered with shutters, Collin turned to Lorraine and Thelma.

"Where's Bill? Where's Athena?"

Their faces didn't reveal anything that could offer him a forewarning.

The sound of a van driving into the compound halted his questions. He rushed outside, back into the rain. The white van, not the bigger one that he'd given to Athena, was now parked. He sloshed his way to the driver's door, pulling it open before Bill had a chance to unbuckle the seat belt.

"Have you seen Athena?"

Bill shook his head. "I've got grandparents of the students. The parents decided to keep the kids, but sent on the older relatives."

"We've got the room." Collin barely heard and had to force himself to concentrate on the details of the conversation that mainly meant nothing to him.

"Thelma and I can help here." Lorraine touched his shoulder. "I'm not sure where she may be headed, but I do know that she had to pick up Marigold."

"That's where the storm will hit first." Collin could hear the water slamming against the seawall. Spray from the force washed over the top like a deadly tease of impending destruction.

Every minute counted. He ran to his office, grabbed the keys to the Land Rover. He hoped the vehicle lived up to its reputation.

"Lorraine, take charge. I'm not sure if the phones will work, but I have my cell phone."

"Be safe," she called, already hurrying to assist one of the elderly guests from the van.

Collin knew that many depended on him and would need his leadership skills to cope with the challenges ahead. He didn't mean to leave Lorraine in the lurch, but Athena, Cicely and Marigold's family were too much at risk to leave them to find their way back to the school.

Her idea had certainly been out of the box. If he hadn't been occupied with the unexpected guests, he could have helped her craft a plan. Or he could have made sure that she had everything she needed. Not being around to get in touch with her was the biggest problem.

As he drove down the road, blinded by the rain, he narrowly avoided cars that had been abandoned. The occupants were nowhere in sight. He hoped that they had reached safety.

He drove the small truck up the mountain. The tires spun, mocking his attempts. Now was not the time for Mother Nature to test his will. He had a goal and nothing short of death was going to stop him.

Finally he got to Marigold's street. Or what was left of it. Mud had created a new landscape, blanketing the neighborhood in red soil. Houses in its path had been relocated past him at the bottom of the mountain. With the continued torrential rain, he didn't trust that the land wouldn't shift further.

But where to look for Athena and Cicely?

He shifted the gear to Reverse and dodged debris that had blown in the way. Then he turned down another side road leading away from the disaster site. A woman stood in the rain staring at an empty spot.

He pulled up next to her. "Get in."

She didn't move.

"Ma'am, we can't stay here. Get in." He honked the horn when she didn't turn.

A little exasperated, he opened the door and ran to her. As he reached for her shoulder, he saw her body shudder. She was openly sobbing. Her focus fastened on the remnants that must have been her home.

"Ma'am, come with me," he said more gently, guiding her back to the truck. Thankfully she didn't resist. "Is there anyone else who needs help?" From the look of the flattened heap, the answer scared him.

She turned into his chest and held on to his shirt in a tight grip. Her grief seeped into his bones, past the dampness of the rain, past the fatigue in his muscles. He waited a few seconds hoping that she would tell him what he dreaded to hear.

"Please, ma'am, is anyone under that heap?"

"I don't know. We were leaving and I had gone down to the end of the road. I sent my brother back for the money I'd left. Then the mud came and covered everything. By the time I got up here, I could barely find my house. And I tried looking for him, but…"

"Go sit in the truck. I'll poke around." Collin helped her in the passenger side.

There wasn't much to dig through, but he'd try to do what he could to reassure her. Slowly he used a stick that he'd found to poke through the mud. He made his way down the road, slipping and sliding, following the trail of debris that was once someone's house. His next steps stopped short.

Partially covered in mud, Athena's van had slid across the road. But more important, the occupants were missing.

Chapter 12

"Marigold! Oh, God, this can't be happening." Athena scooped mud away as fast as she could, flinging it to the side into a slippery new mound of sediment and debris.

She paused only to listen for any telltale signs of where Marigold may be buried.

"Help her!" Luisa grabbed Athena's arm. Her eyes reflected her heightened distress. "You've got to save her." The weeping mother dropped her hands in the mud and wildly dug in the immediate area.

"I've already checked over there." Athena didn't want to waste any time searching for the child.

"Call her name again," Luisa pleaded. "She likes you. She talks about you all the time." Luisa hoisted a large part of the wall from her house, throwing it to one side. She panted from the exertion. "Marigold." This time her voice held more fear than desperation.

Athena hadn't stopped poking several areas with a stick. She wanted a gleam of shiny metal from Marigold's bracelets. Or maybe she would catch a flash of color from her occasional mismatched socks.

"Marigold!" Athena's voice grew hoarse. Her throat ached. But she refused to slow down. Each second was precious.

The rain still pelted onto the landscape, chipping away at the unstable ground.

"She knew you'd come for her." Luisa kneeled, her forearms shoved into the mud up to her elbows. "She liked all the teachers. She'd fight me to go to school. I thought it was a waste of time." She rocked back. Her head bowed. "But, when you came, she turned into a new person. She wasn't just a student anymore." Luisa grunted, as if it was too much effort for any other emotion. "She talked about goals. What does a child at that age know about goals, dreams and passion for life?"

Athena moved to another area. She listened to Luisa, understanding the mother's need to unburden. But Athena refused to talk about Marigold in the past. Considering Luisa was on the verge of a breakdown, she would allow her to continue with her retrospection. On the other hand, Luisa's words provided her with a jolt of motivation to keep going.

Luisa continued, "You are the one to bring Marigold to life. I gave her one sort of life, but you are also responsible for another type of life to her soul." Luisa's voice trembled. "I hope your parents are proud of you."

Athena looked up at the sky, not caring if the rain pounded her skin. If this was the final test to her impulsive act of coming to this island, she refused to buckle. Maybe her parents would be proud. Maybe her grandmother would give her a nod of approval. At this moment, she didn't crave approval. She was in a unique position to be a teacher and a member of various families. The culture allowed for the easy inclusion without blood ties. She relished the acceptance.

"Luisa and Cicely, focus on that part." Athena pointed to a spot where the front door balanced precariously on top of other debris. "We're not giving up." She shifted her position slightly to the right, climbing over appliances. Her legs burned from the injuries she incurred as she navigated through the unfriendly terrain. "Marigold, please answer me, sweetheart." Athena blinked back the tears from frustration.

"Athena! Cicely! It's Collin!" The greeting was said three times.

"Over here." Athena tried to stand but fell in the mud. The wind pushed her back, tossing her as if she weighed nothing. Nothing mattered anymore. Collin had found them. Now he could help her find Marigold.

She struggled to her feet again, pulling against the side of the house to the opening. Everything about the house had blown away except for the partial floor and exterior wall.

"What are you doing?" Collin stared down at her. "Get in the truck."

"Can't. Marigold hid under the house. We can't find her. I'm trying to dig to see if she got buried."

Collin dropped to his knees and started to dig. He didn't have time to get caught up with the details. Time was precious.

"I had her use the house to protect her from the wind and rain. Then Luisa had a meltdown. I couldn't hold both of them. She slipped from my hands."

"We'll find her."

Athena hoped that not only would they find her, but that she would be alive. Her energy doubled as she continued digging.

"I think I have her leg." Collin maintained his hold on the object covered in mud.

Athena brushed off as much as she could; the sock and shoe were still in place. "It's her. Get her out of there."

Collin pulled her out. Thankfully only her mid-section and lower extremities were covered by mud. The rest of her had been under floorboards.

"She's breathing. No outside injuries." He checked her eyes with Athena hovering behind him. "Her eyes are responding."

"Luisa." Athena touched the weeping mother on the side of the cheek. "She's here. She's been found. Come see her."

Marigold stirred. Her eyes fluttered open. She looked straight ahead at a point beyond them.

"My baby." Luisa scooped up the little girl and hugged her. Marigold tried to smile, but her lips trembled. Yet the joy of seeing her mother already reversed the pale countenance to a healthy one. The two embraced.

Athena and Cicely hugged each other.

Another lone soul limped toward them. A man who

had been knocked around by the storm looked dazed. Then the woman in the truck shouted his name. The couple reunited with lots of hugs. As they hugged, Athena choked with emotion.

"I think the rains are letting up. We need to head back before it gets dark." Collin lifted Marigold into the truck.

The little girl's face was beaming up at him. Clearly he had been her hero. Athena helped Luisa, who couldn't stop thanking her for coming to get them.

The woman and her brother, as they eventually figured out, took the ride to a point where the natural disaster had not been so rampant. Another family member arrived in a car and took them. Not until they were driving away did Athena realize that they didn't know their names. But that fact didn't diminish what had just happened. They had saved their lives.

Back at the school, the tearful reunion continued with the rest of the staff. Athena ran home to shower and change into fresh clothes. Now that most of the excitement was over, she was tired and hungry.

"Everyone is settled down for the night. The adults are entertaining the younger ones. Guess we'll know the extent of the damage in the morning," Cicely reported. She joined Athena in the kitchen to make a thick peanut butter and jelly sandwich. "Thanks for turning me onto these," she said, her mouth filled with bread.

"It's even better if you have grape jelly. But I guess we'll make do with the guava jelly."

"Where's Lorraine and Thelma?" Cicely asked.

"They're still over at the school. I think Lorraine is going to stay with everyone."

"Now I feel guilty about jumping into my bed." Cicely groaned, polishing off the last bite of her sandwich.

"Yes, that would look a little insensitive," Athena teased. "I gave mine up to Marigold because we're assuming that she has not suffered any serious injuries. I want her sleeping properly. I'm taking the couch."

"Fine, I'll join Lorraine." Cicely pouted. "I don't recall this being in the fine print."

"Life's surprises are never in the fine print. But you handle them as they come." And this entire trip had certainly done a number on her with the swiftness of certain things.

"I'm going to go tell Lorraine that the shower is free."

"Oh, I didn't know that she was waiting."

"She wasn't. But I was hanging around her a few minutes ago. The shower is free." She wiggled her nose and raised her eyebrows.

"Ah, I get it. Well, you go make your public service announcement. Good luck." Athena placed her dishes in the sink. She was truly exhausted. All the adrenaline rush, fear and imagining the worst now took its toll. But before she crashed for the evening, she had to put fresh linens on her bed for Marigold.

She didn't have much to pick from, but chose a soft pastel blue for the bed. After what happened, she was sure Luisa wouldn't want to leave her daughter's side. Maybe she could ask Lorraine to allow Luisa use of her room. They weren't exactly across the hall from each other, but at least she'd be a few feet down the hall.

The sound of the shower alerted her that Lorraine had caught on to Cicely's hint. At least she could get away with that. Although she and Lorraine had declared a truce to get through today's events, she still felt a strain in their relationship. After the shower, she'd be relaxed and in a good space for when she had to make the request for Luisa.

Once the bed linens had been exchanged, Athena took the sheets to the hamper in a closet near the shower. She heard the water cease and the shower door pop open. Then the doorknob turned. She waited to talk to Lorraine, not wanting to waste one second.

"Oh!" Not only was Collin standing in front of her, but he was standing there with his shirt partly opened, hair damp, with a towel draped casually over his arm.

"Sorry, I ran over here for a quick shower because there is a long line in the men's house. And the shower in the school building was being used. I had to get the mud off."

"No problem. I understand." She shifted from one foot to the next. She'd done her part to keep the depth of her feelings for him a secret. She hid it from her coworkers. She hid it from him and she didn't want to reflect on her feelings.

"Are you still angry with me?"

"Why?"

"When you came to the house…?"

"I figure you had something important going on."

He nodded.

"You can use my room to finish dressing." She bit down on her disappointment that he didn't elaborate or provide any further explanation.

"Thanks." He went to her room, then hesitated in

front of the door. "Don't jump to conclusions, okay? Give me a chance."

Now was the time for no-holds-barred honesty. "Collin, I'm more than the woman you sleep with. I'm not a dirty little secret. Your whole life is a mystery and shouldn't have to be. I'm not the enemy."

He pulled her close. His mouth touched hers before she had time to pull away. He kissed her, the urgency pouring through his very touch. If she stayed this way, enjoying the stroke of his tongue, he would take control of her thoughts and mind.

"No. I can't. We can't bury whatever is between us with your kisses." She laid her forehead against his chest. His heartbeat matched hers, pounding away at a steady clip.

The smallest act between them had a gigantic reaction. Their energy grew exponentially, recharging with every kiss, embrace or time spent making love.

"I can't resist you."

"That may be true." She sighed. "I know it's true, but that doesn't make it all right."

"You have to trust me."

She looked up into his face. Those dark eyes that had a depth within them had captured her heart. She gasped.

"What is it?"

"Nothing." None of her sorority sisters had explained that falling in love had such power. She'd seen how they had reacted, but chalked it up to the dopiness that came when in a new relationship. She'd also chalked it up to that lustful period when either side couldn't keep their hands off the other.

"I can see that you're not happy with me," Collin stated.

"I have to go to see to Marigold."

He raised her chin with the crook of his finger.

Athena focused on the fact that he was hiding something from her to break the effect. She blinked, keeping her eyes closed for a second. Mentally she wiped away his words, empty promises, that held no future. If he was mixed up in anything shady, he could not be part of her life. She didn't want to be one of those women who were too blind to see the obvious.

Three months on the job and her career plans had taken a slight detour. She couldn't continue to see him as much as she had pushed for all this to happen. Her heart wasn't supposed to be compromised. Maybe her inexperience at falling in love had led her to this uncomfortable rocky place where every turn jabbed at her. But he seemed so sincere about this special school and the community he served.

"You don't want to kiss me," he remarked.

She shook her head, twisting her chin out of his hold.

"I think that you're…"

"Collin, you're needed at the school. One of the parents may need to be taken to the hospital. And there's a man waiting for you." Lorraine stood at the beginning of the hall.

"A man?"

"Kitchner."

"Damn!" Collin turned to say something, but shook his head. "If the weather has let up, Lorraine, get Bill to take the person to the hospital."

She nodded, but didn't turn to leave. Instead she

looked at Athena and then at Collin. Her cool blue eyes held judgment.

"Athena, when you're done in here, there is work to be done with our guests," Lorraine shouted.

Athena knew she stated the obvious, but the ugliness in her tone provided the undercurrent that Lorraine was furious. She didn't know how much the woman had witnessed or listened to, but she'd have to deal with the consequences and have a heart-to-heart.

"I'll be there." Athena waited until Collin walked ahead, before she also exited.

Over at the school, most had settled in for the night. The dinner of soup, bread and cookies had been cleared away. Some of the younger children still snacked on crackers and milk.

Athena stopped to talk to everyone as she passed. Despite the hectic pace of the rescue mission and the unexpected number and range of guests, she was happy as she looked over the small sea of faces.

"You know you're going to have tell me what's up with you and the boss?"

Athena spun around to see Cicely grinning at her. She shook her head. This was not the time. And after tonight, there was nothing between the boss and her. She had to return to the plain facts to survive. Collin was her boss, nothing else.

"Okay, I can see that you're not in the best of mood. Did Lorraine say something? I saw her heading to the house. I tried to stop her, but she had an objective and wasn't going to be denied."

"It was like breathing in the fire from a dragon. She probably would have stomped me down if she could."

Cicely laughed. But Athena really couldn't find humor in the situation.

She worked for another hour and then decided to take the first shift in keeping watch over everyone. Thankfully with so many of them, she only had a two-hour shift. Then she could escape to her makeshift bed on the living-room couch.

Cicely opted to play cards for a little while with the guys. Lorraine and Thelma had disappeared. But Athena didn't complain about that. She much preferred it that way.

Now that things had calmed down, her mind drifted to Collin and the mysterious Kitchner.

Curious to see if Collin had left, she walked toward his office. The door had to be open because a shaft of light lit the otherwise semidark hallway. She slowed her approach, easing against the wall. Muffled voices filtered back to her.

She stepped closer. This time she would find out even if it meant getting caught. She wanted evidence that Collin hadn't taken a desperate act to sell his soul to Kitchner.

"You refuse everything from me as if I was contagious. I have never crossed your path. I have never stabbed you in the back. I only want to help you." The man who had to be Kitchner had a thick, distinctively raspy voice, perfect for a bad guy. Instead of being comforted by the tone, Athena imagined the slick wiliness of a snake.

"This is my school. I have worked hard for it. You cannot come in here and try to buy me."

"Buy you? I wanted this school here. I wanted these children to have a future. Now that you've got a couple years under your belt, you want to act as if you can put distance from me."

"I'm tired. We keep going around in circles." Collin's voice bore the fatigue that had hit all of them. The volume of his voice lowered and Athena had to step closer to hear. "I don't need your money."

"I'm not giving you money. I have computers, overhead LCD equipment, educational computer software. You say the word and they will be delivered."

"I'm not answering you tonight."

"At least that's better than your shutting the door in my face. You'd better let me help you, protect what you've got, rather than deal with the bosses. I can control them only up to a point. You're giving people hope and that's a dangerous thing."

"Well, that must not earn you any points either."

"You're right. And one day there will come a time when I have to pay my dues."

Athena heard the chair push back, grating against the floor, providing a loud warning that she had to move. She backed up and bumped into someone.

Her scream died when she saw Lorraine standing there, leaning against the wall. She didn't know what to say.

"Why are you here?" Athena was tired of Lorraine's creepy, stalker attitude.

"Looks like we're doing the same thing."

"You are acting so weird. More than usual," Athena replied.

"I suppose you're acting the same way you used to when you first got here. The American girl-next-door seems to have taken a trip to the wild side. Before your arrival, we had a mission. We stuck to it. Collin didn't have side interests and wasn't distracted."

"I'm a distraction?"

"You don't need me to answer that. You may be stupid, but not that stupid."

"Is it that you wish you were in my shoes?"

"Shut up."

"Oh, my God, that's it, isn't it?" Athena covered her mouth with her hand. "You're in love with Collin?" she whispered.

"What's going on out here?" Collin stepped in the hallway, but closed the door. "Is something wrong?"

Athena didn't respond. The revelation almost bowled her over. Lorraine's face was still flushed an angry red. Her eyes were bright and shimmering as if she would fall apart if someone said the wrong thing. Athena saw her hands close and open and she took a step forward.

"Athena, we need to talk. Can you stick around?"

And Lorraine took a step back. Her hands closed into fists and didn't reopen. Her gaze shifted to Athena and a coldness crept in and stayed there. She spun on her heel and left.

"What's going on?"

Athena looked at the stiff retreat of her coworker. She hated that Lorraine's secret feelings had to surface in such a cold, brutal manner.

"Athena?" Collin called.

"You know, I think that I'd better get going. We can talk tomorrow."

"Let's talk tonight. I'm ready to talk."

"Excuse me. Collin, I have to leave." The man who must be Kitchner stepped into the hallway next to Collin. He glanced to Athena, his eyes squinted, examining her. "Are you one of the teachers?"

Athena nodded. She didn't care for his tone, but considering who he was and what he was capable of doing to her, she answered. Now he offered his hand. She couldn't ignore it without consequences. Already she'd pegged him with guns strapped all over his body and bodyguards to finish the job. She placed her hand in his.

"What's your name?" He hadn't released her hand.

"Athena Crawford."

"Ah." A broad smile was bestowed upon her. "I've heard of your strides with our local youth. I am in your debt, young lady." He bowed before releasing her hand.

She tried not to wipe her hand clean on her clothes. His leering smile felt like an oil slick ran through her system. She hoped that Collin would intervene, but he merely stared at the older man. In her opinion, he looked uncomfortable and antsy.

"Mr. Kitchner, I have to be going. I'll leave you to finish chatting with Collin."

"My dear, I wish I had the stamina to keep talking to Collin. Alas, I have to be on my way. There may be others in need of my help." He placed the handle of a large umbrella on his forearm. "Collin, don't let your pride get in your way."

He walked away, leaving Athena with Collin.

She didn't wait long, but hurried down the hallway, too, making her exit. In doing so, she ignored Collin calling to her.

The tropical storm lasted three days and had done millions of dollars of damage on the island. Collin counted the school lucky not to have suffered major structural damage and nothing had been destroyed.

Almost everything had returned to normal. Students were back in classes. His staff was performing at optimum standards. He was finally getting caught up on writing proposals for more grants. Their efforts had made it in the nation's newspapers with a prominent photo of the staff and Marigold's family.

"Mr. Winslow, here's your mail." Clarissa handed him the letters already opened for his convenience. She hovered, very much unlike her.

"Is something wrong?" He took the mail, but kept his focus on her.

Clarissa, meanwhile, hadn't shifted her gaze from his face. Her expression puzzled him. He looked down at the envelope with various international postage and stamps. From the return address, he determined that the letter was from the parent organization of the teachers program located in France. "Are you going to tell me what's in the letter?"

She shook her head and backed out.

Collin took a deep breath and shook the letter into his hand. He opened the brief typewritten note. Its contents created a boulder-size heartburn. His head roared in protest. When he was finished, he set it down on the desk and leaned back in the chair.

Clarissa eased back into his office. Her actions reminded him of a mouse, hovering but willing to run if necessary.

"Looks like we're about to get audited. Did any e-mails about this come in?" Collin's mind raced through the potential outcome to the contents.

She nodded. "There will be Dominique Gaston and two others arriving today. She wants to interview the entire staff and have access to all documents."

"Someone complained." He reiterated the letter's message.

"Or accused."

"You know about this?" Clarissa always knew the gossip around the school grounds.

"Maybe."

"Talk." He needed to know every tiny detail of the rumors that had to be swirling.

"Someone wrote a complaint to the European headquarters."

"A complaint? One of the parents?"

She shook her head. "It was sort of an accusation."

"Accusing who of what? This letter doesn't provide much detail."

"You of dealing with organized crime."

"What?" Collin erupted in a long string of curses.

Clarissa eyes grew wide.

"Do you know who did this?"

She stayed silent. Her head dropped on her chest.

"Don't you dare hold anything back." Collin hadn't

felt such rage with his school or staff. Plus he hadn't been able to make headway with Athena. She'd gone very professional and refused to remain in any room with him. He refused to think that it was over, but he certainly missed her. Now someone had betrayed him. "If you don't tell me, you can pack your things and leave."

"I—I am sorry. I only just heard about this. But I didn't know how to tell you. Then the letter arrived. What will you do?"

"Who is it?" he said through gritted teeth.

"Lorraine."

Chapter 13

Dominique Gaston, director of employee relations, arrived with her own driver in a two-car caravan. Her itinerary had been e-mailed to the office. Collin waited in the common area at the precise time. The staff was busy with classes. He saw no reason to pull them from their duties or close the school for the day. They needed to see that their investigation wasn't going to change normal procedure.

The most difficult part in this ugly, stressful play was to continue working with Lorraine without revealing what he'd learned. Try as he might, he couldn't figure out why she disliked him enough to levy a false accusation. She never presented her question to him. However, worry snaked through him. Guilt had a way of sticking because the victim happened to be in the vicinity.

But he wasn't giving up without a fight.

The car stopped in front of him and he stepped forward to open the door, but the driver beat him to the task. Instead he waited for the director to emerge like a queen.

"Good morning, Dominique."

"Collin, how do you do?" Her French accent swirled around the words. However, the accent didn't dilute the cool greeting. "These are the financial analysts who will be checking everything. I will take care of the other matters."

"Other matters?" Collin almost choked. There was more than one issue.

"We'll talk inside." Dressed in a black pantsuit and crisp white shirt, she was pure business. Her cool demeanor had to be physical because she didn't appear mussed or affected by the heat.

Collin held open the entrance door for her small army to enter. Clarissa stood off to the side, looking as if she was ready to melt into the wall. She signaled to Collin, who nodded.

"My office is ahead." He walked forward to lead the group to his office. His assistant came in with a tray laden with water, tea, finger sandwiches and cookies. "This is Clarissa."

"Good to meet you. You are the first one on the list to be interviewed."

"Interviewed? Mr. Winslow?" Clarissa looked as if she needed to be rescued.

"Clarissa, I'm in charge here. I'm conducting interviews of the entire staff. Be available in an hour." Dominique paused. "You can leave now."

Collin felt sorry for the young woman, who looked ready to pass out from the stress. With her hasty exit, he was sure that she ran to the others to explain, probably with nervous embellishment.

Dominique closed his door and then surveyed his office. Her presence felt oppressive and set his nerves on edge. He remained standing, observing her as she made her rounds of the entire office, flipping through his in-box and then taking his chair to sit.

"I think that I've been patient about this investigation of my character. And no one has answered my question to reveal any information. I don't understand how an accusation warrants a personal visit." This situation was nightmarish. Dominique wasn't going to come in, snap her fingers and destroy what he and his staff had built.

Dominique slid her fingers along the outer edge of his desk. She examined her fingers before rubbing them together to dislodge the dust. Collin wondered if he was about to be accused of a third thing—poor housekeeping.

"Collin, the nature of the accusations is very important and is the basis for immediate dismissal if found to be true. I want to believe that there is some big mistake. But there are other improprieties that must be checked into."

"Like what?" Although he should be delighted that she was now explaining the weird circumstances, he didn't like the vague improprieties.

"I am here for only two days. I have no desire to be in this hot place for any longer. We should find what we need to know in that time. And you'll have my recommendation before I leave."

"Find? Good grief, could you be any more vague? By the way, where are you staying?"

"I'll be in the city. My arrangements have already been made."

Collin took the chair on the other side of his desk. He didn't like the feeling of being on the defensive, but his future was in shreds. Even if he was cleared, the stigma had now been created. His every move would be second-guessed.

"What is the other accusation?"

"That you have had improper relations with a member of your staff."

He swore that her words had the effect of a cold hand around his heart, squeezing until he passed out.

"And from the feigned horrified expression, I guess that is true. Well, that will cut my investigation short. Who is it?"

"Ask your snitch." Collin had had enough. He wasn't dragging Athena into this.

"Actually the person did provide a name. Just checking to see if the name you reveal matches what was in the letter."

"And do I get a chance to confront the accuser?"

"All in due time. We have to protect the person's rights, too."

"And what about mine? Was it so easy after everything I've accomplished here to think that I'd done these things?"

"Actually I was coming here, anyway, but then these issues popped up. Kind of like the perfect storm."

"And what did you initially want?" Collin rubbed his

head, wondering how quickly his life seemed shot to pieces.

"To offer you a post at the headquarters in France." She flipped her hair. "But these other matters have to be cleared."

Moving from the field to the home office may sound ideal in the next five years, but he didn't join the organization aiming for the top of the mountain. A cushy desk job in Europe didn't stoke his passion to work elbow to elbow with teachers and children.

"I'm going to update my staff. Then I'm going to leave the premises while you continue with your witch hunt."

"Don't go too far. I'll be interviewing you and your consenting staff member tomorrow morning."

Collin slammed his office door closed. He was angry enough to punch a hole in the wall. He paced the hallway, trying to focus on what to do. Then he decided that he had to talk to Lorraine. He wanted answers.

Athena sat at the table listening to Clarissa fill them in on the goings-on. They were all there in the teachers' lounge, except for Lorraine. When the office assistant mentioned who accused Collin, the remaining teachers were shocked. A few tempers escalated to anger because of their betrayed feelings.

With her last class for the day dismissed, Athena was grateful for the early afternoon to herself. She had to find Collin to see how he was doing. Despite their disagreement, she couldn't evict him from her heart. If the staff were unsettled, then she knew he had to feel low. She headed for his office.

She knocked and popped her head in.

"Come in."

Athena frowned, clearly not expecting a stranger's voice dripping with a French accent. She entered the office, a little tentative.

"Good to see you. Which one are you?"

"Athena Crawford." From the way this woman dressed and had taken over Collin's desk, she figured this was the representative wreaking havoc. If her demeanor didn't slice her victim to shreds, then the sharp fashion statement and makeup with precision application could perform the deed. Every facial feature was sharp, pointed, angular and defined.

"Do come in. I'm looking forward to talking with you in the morning."

"Why do you need to talk to me? If this is about Collin, then I have nothing to say."

"I bet you don't. You are the only one who is so close to Collin that you would know everything."

"I'm not a snitch."

"No, but you are an employee who could be dishonorably discharged and sent back to the States."

Athena wanted to run out of the office, but fought to stay calm. She had done nothing to warrant a dishonorable discharge.

"Let me give you a heads-up for your interview tomorrow." Dominique propped her chin. Her red nails heightened the feeling of danger. "We'll be talking about Collin's interaction with Kitchner."

"I don't know anything about that. I never dealt with him."

"You did meet him, though."

"Yes," Athena hissed.

"We'll get into that a bit more tomorrow."

"May I go?"

"Sure." Dominique watched her, making her feel like a mouse being toyed with by a cat, a sneaky one.

As she left, she sensed that there was more that the woman wanted to say. Now she had the evening to think about what the woman really wanted. She didn't know whether she should dress as if she was on an interview or casual for the plane ride home.

Unease blanketed the school yard. Teachers and other staff created tiny huddles sifting over the swirling information. Still there was no sign of Lorraine. Athena hadn't checked the house, but really didn't want to. Her coworker had effectively sabotaged one career, maybe others.

Cicely looked miserable as she chatted with Thelma. They both looked over at Athena before shifting away their gazes. Athena slowed her approach. She'd planned to sit in their huddle and chat about everything. The last thing she expected was an outright rejection. She considered them, especially Cicely, her bud. Not only did they avoid eye contact, but now they'd turned their backs on her. If they treated her this way, had they been equally nasty to Collin?

She went to her room and packed an overnight bag. Staying on-site held no pleasure. Thankfully no one wanted to be bothered and stayed away from her.

Athena drove off the property, planning to go into town and reserve a room at a hotel. Halfway there, she remembered Clarissa mentioning that Dominique and her crew would be staying in town. The small island buzzed with the news of the important arrivals and the boisterous entourage. There was a slim chance that she would run into the barracuda of a woman, but she didn't need that stress.

Instead she turned the car north and followed the familiar streets to Collin's house. She pulled up in the driveway and parked. He was on the veranda, feet up, leaning back with his eyes closed.

She stood at the bottom of the steps, waiting for him to acknowledge her. But instead he stared out into the darkness. The atmosphere didn't feel good. She slowly climbed the stairs, surveying the area where he sat. The glass in his hand partly filled with amber-colored liquid spoke volumes. She wondered how much had been in the glass.

"Collin?" She walked in front of him, waiting for his acknowledgment.

Slowly he turned to her. A wan smile crossed his face.

"You're looking too sad." She took the empty seat next to him. She raised his arm over her head and nestled under his arm.

"And that changed your mind about me?"

"Actually I've set aside my feelings," Athena explained.

"Really?"

"Yes, really. This could mean a nasty end—here and in the courts."

Collin nodded, no longer talking. His expression grew pensive.

"I know we've had our issues. But I'm here."

They sat quietly looking out in the dark. He never picked up his glass. He didn't speak to her. But when his thumb stroked her arm, she knew that she offered him some measure of comfort.

"Tomorrow is going to be hell for you."

His voice breaking the silence startled her.

"Why do you say that? I'm sure it's not going to be an easy day for you, either."

"Oh, baby, you don't know, do you?"

"You're being accused. That Dominique woman wanted to know if I'd met Kitchner. She's a frigid nimrod."

"Don't underestimate her. I can't believe that it's over."

"Don't say that. It's not over." Athena rose up, seeing the tortured mask. "Let's go inside."

"Are you staying with me?"

She pushed away from him and went to her car. He followed her. As she opened the door, he grabbed her arm. "Please don't go. I promise that I won't touch you. But I want you to stay. I'll be satisfied with that. Need a friendly face around me."

"Liar!" she accused, smiling. Then she reached in for her overnight bag. "You'd better not be satisfied with me just being in the house. I don't want depressing love-making." She strutted back to the house, leaving a very stunned Collin standing in the driveway. "Are you coming?"

"Thank you for coming."

She smiled and they walked in arm-in-arm. "I'll go take a shower. Pour me a glass of wine, will you. I need to unwind."

"Will do."

By the time she came out the wine had been poured.

Candles flickered around the room. He sat on his side of the bed with pillows propped behind him.

"You look damn good." He patted the spot next to him.

"I'm here and you still look sad. What's up with that?" She teased, poking his rib.

"Kitchner isn't the only problem."

"There's more?" Athena pushed herself up. She didn't realize that there would be more issues. Had she jumped to a conclusion that Collin was free of guilt? She listened keenly.

"They know about us."

"Us?"

"Our improper behavior has been documented."

"Damn."

"I know."

Athena was truly sorry that someone had accused Collin of improper behavior. What they shared wasn't improper and they were careful to keep it away from the school. Yet that hadn't been enough.

"Do you know who is accusing you?"

He nodded. "Clarissa is a wealth of information. The woman sees all and knows all. I'm convinced that she's got spy cameras and listening devices all over the property."

"What? Who? Is it someone we know?"

He nodded.

Athena closed her eyes, mentally running through the faces of everyone around her. The only person who had treated her like dirt was Lorraine. Yet she remembered how Cicely and Thelma had turned away from her.

"I bet Lorraine did this," she accused.

He nodded.

Athena thought about the impact of what they'd done. Although she wanted to throttle the woman, how could she? They had broken the rules. As much as she wanted a legitimate, above-the-board relationship with Collin, she had still contributed to their sorry state of affairs.

Yet after all of that and what she suspected would come out tomorrow, she refused to feel any remorse. She had wanted Collin more than her sanity. They had shared a wonderful time together and she still wanted more.

"Baby, tomorrow, I will explain everything in my life. I want you standing next to me, as my witness," Collin reassured her.

"I will be at your side. And they will be disappointed that there isn't any drama between us. Because we are being accused, we might as well enjoy the time we have together."

"You're such a fighter," he teased.

"And you're a visionary."

"Come here." Collin opened his arms, inviting her into his embrace.

Athena snuggled into the firm chest, resting her forehead just under his chin.

"I love you."

Athena dared to hope that she had not imagined the words that she wanted to hear above the rest. "Say it again," she whispered.

"Athena Crawford, I love you."

Chapter 14

Athena slid down on the bed. The pillows surrounded her body in a soft cocoon. Collin propped himself with one arm while unbuttoning her nightshirt. The baby blue color complemented her skin tone. When he was done, he flicked each shirt panel to either side of her, leaving her stomach bare.

His mouth touched her stomach, making her hiss. He laid his arms on either side of her body, kissing the bared skin. Her body contorted and relaxed with each kiss.

"What is that sexy scent you use?" His lips brushed against her stomach.

"It's old vanilla bean. I have a bunch of products in that scent."

"Mmm." He finger-walked his hand up her stomach

and cupped her breast. His fingers tweaked one nipple then the other into puckered tips.

She moaned, tilting her body toward his mouth to quench the thirst for what he had to offer. Her hands roved through his hair and down his face. She wanted to remember every nuance, every feature because she didn't know what would happen to them after tomorrow. But whatever did happen, she was at peace with her feelings for him.

"Baby, let's make love until we pass out in each other's arms."

"Sleep is overrated," she joked, slipping out from under him.

"Where are you going?"

"Close your eyes," she whispered.

"Oh, are we going to get kinky?"

"Stop grinning like a schoolboy." She reached for a tie and tied it around his face, blinding him. "We're going to play a game."

"Does this involve food? Do I get to do a taste test?"

She kissed his ear, moving away when he tried to kiss her back. "No food involved…I think."

He reached for her and she scooted away with only the brush of his fingers flickering down her leg.

"We'll play Marco Polo. I'll tell you when you're hot," she explained.

"But you get to decide."

"Not really. Your body will decide when it's really hot."

"I'm ready now," Collin whined.

"I'm sure you are." She kissed his bare shoulder again, ducking out of reach of his captive embrace.

"Okay, I'll play along."

"Count to ten. You don't have to worry about going outside of the bedroom. I don't want you breaking your neck on the stairs." Athena giggled.

"One. Two. Three…"

Athena slipped past him and headed for the wardrobe. She stood among the clothes.

"Ten!" Collin stood up from the bed. "Marco."

"Polo," she whispered. She watched him walk around with arms outstretched.

"Marco!"

"Polo." She eased back in between the clothes as he raised his chin. She looked closely to see if he could, but when he stubbed his toe, she knew that he couldn't see.

"Marco. Athena, this isn't fun."

"Polo." She dropped to the floor of the closet, watching his legs swing into view. The man was so beautiful in clothes and definitely out of them.

He sniffed the air. So that was what he'd been doing every time he held up his head.

Then suddenly he dropped to the floor, pulled off his tie, and grabbed her in a bear hug. "You're not getting away."

"Were you peeking?" she said breathlessly. She couldn't stop giggling when he scooped her up and set her on the bed.

"I told you that vanilla bean is memorable. Plus I don't like playing with my food when I'm hungry. So I certainly don't want to be teased when my sexual hunger is roaring for food."

She slid her hands over his butt cheeks that were

muscularly hard. She massaged him and drew her hands to the front to stroke him.

Collin's voice hitched and his speech came out stilted. She grinned, turning up the tricks that her fingers did on him.

"If it's to be all night, you need to stop."

She complied and lay back spread-eagled.

"Oh, no." He dropped on all fours in front of her. "Why can't you play fair?"

She grinned.

"Oh, so it's going to be like that."

She wiggled out from under him, waited for him to put on the latex and mounted. "Yep, it's like that now."

He writhed under her, heightening sensations between her legs. His hands cupped and teased her breasts. Because she kept them away from his eager mouth, he sat holding her in place. Then he stood and positioned her back against the wall.

Her feet didn't touch the ground. All she could do was hold his head against her chest. Her breasts crushed against him, sensitive to the texture of his chest.

Wrapping her feet around his butt invited him in farther. She welcomed his entry, matching each movement. The energy built, soared, zoomed to the summit where they hovered, coasting, catching their breaths.

Perspiration moistened their bodies, heralding the power of their union. Athena wanted every part of Collin. There was desperation in their lovemaking tonight. The unknown had its own attraction.

"Hold on, baby."

She did as she was told. Her fingers tightened their

grasp of him. Her body quivered, the only warning that she was about to explode.

"Come with me," she begged.

"Always," he answered.

Each body writhed and grinded against the other. Athena held on to his shoulders, trying to talk but not managing. Her body experienced multiple orgasms that drained energy from all over. Now her muscles trembled from the exertion.

Her feet finally touched the floor, testing the hard surface. She didn't know how Collin managed to keep her in the air for that length of time, but being grounded certainly wasn't necessary to feel the passion.

"I think we may miss the sunrise. It's only two o'clock. Do you have the stamina?"

"Be optimistic. You never know what could happen when the spirit is willing." Athena crawled into bed weak with satisfaction.

Collin cleaned up and rejoined her in the bed. "We have a rough go at it tomorrow. But don't allow your mind to prejudge the situation. Have faith in me."

"Of course." She kissed him. Maybe a quick prayer would help, too. She hoped that she could deliver on her promise about having faith.

From the time that Collin opened his eyes, he was tense. He awoke in the morning thinking that he would be relaxed after their marathon lovemaking session. Instead he was going through all the possible questions and how he would answer each.

He looked over at Athena, who was still asleep. He

wished that he'd rehearsed her responses. Now it was too late. Plus if he worked so hard to craft his answers, she would have doubts about his truth.

A cold shower, two cups of coffee and another one for the road, he still wasn't ready for what lay ahead. Athena sat quietly in the passenger seat lost in her own thoughts.

"I hope that sad look isn't because of me."

She smiled and touched his cheek. "I feel like we're walking into the lion's den."

"That would be lioness."

"She's so intimidating. I feel like an underdressed adolescent schoolgirl around her." She pulled down the visor and dabbed at the corner of her lips.

"You look fantastic. In my opinion, you didn't need the makeup. Or the suit. You look professional no matter what you wear."

"I love the fact that you flatter me." She stretched over and kissed him close to his ear.

"No lipstick on the collar. You're really trying to get me strung up."

"Do you think that they will interview us separately?"

He nodded. "But we have nothing to hide."

She turned away toward the window.

"Athena, do you think that I have something to hide?"

"The Kitchner person. He was at your house." She looked down at her lap. "And then he was at the school. I listened at the door. That's how Lorraine caught me."

Collin recalled both incidents. He shook his head. His actions had created that wedge between them when that was so far from what he'd intended.

They drove in silence to the school. Not only was he

ready to be interviewed, but he wanted his staff sitting in the room with him. They were a team. Had successfully brought the vision to fruition. And he was going to fight to keep it going.

When they arrived at the school together, everyone stared. He guided Athena into his office. Dominique was already there. And she had dressed the part.

Her hair was severely pulled back. Whatever she'd put on it shined under the light. The black pantsuit had been changed for a pencil-thin, sleeveless black dress with black pumps. She seemed to embrace her judiciary role with sinister enthusiasm.

"Before we begin, I want my staff present for the discussion about my organized crimes connection."

"You're making demands?"

"Yes. I have not asked for anything as my reputation has been shredded. But I want a chance to have my say in front of my staff."

"Oh, this I have to hear. Because I have the research on Kitchner." She slammed her hand on a ream of paper. "There is no way that this man and you should have any ties." She pressed the intercom and requested the staff to come to the small meeting room connected to his office.

Collin didn't waver from his decision to tell everything and to tell his staff. However, the events still left him a bit shaky and very angry. His mouth felt dry and he craved a cup of cold water. In five minutes this would be over. And that's what he kept telling himself to stop from deliberating about everything he would reveal.

"I'm here for you. I believe in you." Athena rubbed his back before taking her seat.

The tender exchanged wasn't lost on Dominique, who wrote in her pad.

The staff filed in. Lorraine came in last and sat away from the group. From the redness around her eyes and blotchy skin, he figured that she'd been crying. He tried to get her to look at him, but she kept her gaze lowered. Her arms were crossed in front of her. He knew that her defenses were up.

"Collin, would you care to begin?"

Collin stepped away from Athena. What he had to say was separate from her. He wanted each of his staff to listen to him and not get confused about her presence or loyalty.

"I have been accused of fraternizing with organized crime. As you know when we chose this location, we were entering their territory. We were here to save a generation of kids who had a bleak future. And we were met with resistance. We had to prove ourselves. We had to earn respect and trust. We talked to parents who were role models. We talked to those who were abusive and intervened when we could. We mixed in with the good and bad of society with the common goal of making this school work and be a success."

"So the end justified your dealing with people who are heads of prostitution rings, dealing drugs, just the scourge of the earth." Dominique rattled off the items on her manicured fingers.

Collin looked her right in the eye, waiting for her to finish.

"Let him speak." Lorraine finally looked at him. "I want to hear what he has to say."

"Yes," the staff echoed.

"I was born and grew up on this island. But I was lucky enough to go to America and finish high school and then go on to college. All that time, I didn't forget where I came from. I was tempted to work with big well-funded nonprofits. The lifestyle drew me in, but I'd made a promise to my parents that I would lift up another child. My family broke apart when I was a child, but my mother stayed here. It was her brothers, my uncles, who gave me that start." He paused. His heartbeat pounded dully in his head.

"Go on, sweetheart."

"The police commissioner is my uncle. And Kitchner is my uncle."

"Is this true?" Dominique's cool mask of indifference slipped away and she was struck speechless.

"My uncles funded my college education. When my head was up in the clouds thinking of settling in America, Kitchner, his nickname, begged me to come back and start the school. He offered money, but I didn't take it. I had money of my own that I invested. Instead he forced his competitors to back off and give us a window to thrive. This house is from a former drug dealer. One of the competitors that my uncle strongly suggested should provide us with the building. Times have changed and not necessarily for the better. Competitors are in a power struggle and Kitchner may get pulled in. To make matters worse, our success hasn't helped raise our profile. Now they want property. Now that we are a success, they are pressuring. Once off the island, my uncle, the police commissioner, has been able to get funding for the U.S. DEA intervention. The people aren't passively tolerating the thugs. Yes, my uncle will have to pay for his misdeeds. And I'm sure he'll try to negotiate his way with the DEA. But I tried to do what I could without his money and influence."

"I didn't know," Lorraine said.

"I worked hard not to let anyone know." He looked down at Athena, hoping that she would understand. Her answering smile set his mind at ease. "Would I really have gotten the financing for the school if my family connections were known? Would the international program want to be associated with me?"

Dominique clearly looked irritated. "Well, I will take the circumstances under consideration. Let's take a short break. Then, Collin, see me back in my office."

"You mean *my* office."

Silence descended. All eyes focused on Collin.

Dominique walked out, but she had to have heard the loud roar of laughter and applause as the door closed.

Collin finished the meeting with his staff, addressing any further concerns. Collin turned to his staff. His pride swelled, buoyed by their loyalty. "I am humbled by your support."

Chapter 15

After the break, Collin geared up his mind to handle the next matter of concern. He may have cleared things up but he didn't know what the final outcome would be. Dominique wouldn't entertain any sidebar conversation with him.

"Let's get this over with." Athena slipped her arm through his and gave him a comforting squeeze.

"I'm glad you're at my side. You give me strength to deal with my convictions." He opened his hand and waited for her slender one to slip into his grasp.

Slow and deliberate they walked together into Collin's office. Dominique had already started packing the files, along with the stack of paper that they'd copied for the audit.

"Oh, I see that you've come as comrade-in-arms, quite literally." She indicated the chair. "Have a seat."

Collin allowed Athena to sit, but he remained standing. The past twenty-fours had been hellish. But with his woman at his side, a night of sweet loving and his integrity intact, he no longer feared his fate. He locked gazes with Dominique to let her know the show was over.

She gave a slight nod, but he saw her mouth tighten; the blast of red lip color looked like an ink blot.

"Let's get started. I'll begin with Athena. Collin, you can leave the room."

"No, I'm going to stay." He placed a hand on Athena's shoulder, sending as much reassurance to her.

"As you wish."

"Athena, there has been accusation levied against you and your boss of improper behavior. Is that true?"

"I-in…"

"There is no policy on file," Collin piped up.

"There is sexual harassment."

"It certainly was not harassment." Athena leaned forward, but Collin kept his hand on her shoulder to ease her back.

He knew that Dominique relished raising the drama and making her subject feel out of control. Athena had to recognize the rules of the game to survive her. But he wouldn't let the situation get to that point.

"So you're admitting that there were relations?"

"Yes," Athena answered.

"Was it out in the open?"

"No."

"Then it was improper. You knew it was improper, otherwise you wouldn't have had to have secret meetings."

"I didn't want anyone to know," Athena explained.

"Usually the sign of someone who has done wrong." Dominique flipped open a file and trailed her finger down a paper covered with writing. She stopped midpoint and then looked up.

"Collin, because you insist on being here, I might as well bring you into the conversation."

"Oh, is that what this is? I would have tossed it up there with inquisition."

"Watch it," she warned. Her eyes sparkled with open hostility. "Do you feel that in your capacity as head of this school, you should have been fraternizing with the staff?"

"It was not my intent."

"But you didn't stop it. Was there no guilt? No remorse?"

Collin didn't want to reveal the inner dialogue. She didn't deserve to know how much he battled with his feelings. She would have no respect of the complexity of emotions.

"I love him," Athena said with a small but clear voice.

Dominique's eyes flashed down to Athena. Then she pushed back the chair and walked in front of the desk. Her scrutiny flickered over him, but settled back on Athena, who kept her gaze straight ahead.

"Four years ago, I was an intern for this organization in America. Everything about the country dazzled me. Big cities. People not afraid of showing their emotions. Feeling uninhibited. I loved the American lifestyle," Dominique reminisced.

Collin knew where she was going with this as she coaxed them along her path.

"Then I met a man, a young man, still wet behind the ears with his mother's milk. I could barely speak English. But we made quite the couple."

Collin felt the tightness of Athena's body. She realized there was about to be an untimely revelation.

"I was in love. We were going to conquer the world. We were going to save it. So many dreams thrown up in the air before crashing down." She sighed. "Chalk it up to youth." Dominique stopped pacing, staring hard at Collin. He didn't have a problem meeting her attempts to intimidate. However, he did cringe at the sight of Athena pinching the bridge of her nose. Her mouth drew into a tight line. He hoped that she trusted him.

"I went back to France, but we kept in touch. And then I was hired by the organization. But the young man who had melted my heart, well, I outgrew him. I'm a complex being, but we women are, aren't we?" She glanced down at Athena, as if waiting for her to answer. With a shrug, she continued, "I have learned not to throw out love with such careless abandon. Use what you have to get what your heart desires, but move on. Move up. I did and look what it's got me." She stood and walked over to Collin. Despite her cool façade, her anger bristled off her.

"Who broke your heart to make you so cold?" Athena interrupted.

"A stupid boy with too many ideals. Now I only go after men." She took a deep breath. "You love him, right?"

Athena nodded.

"And you love her, right?"

"More than this job."

Athena gasped.

"More than the opportunity to come back to France with me."

"Collin?" Athena looked up at him.

"This is home. This is my job."

"I'm offering you a life's rope. Opportunities such as what I'm presenting don't come around often. I can make you a star in this organization." Dominique spoke as if only him and her existed.

"Your offer of a rope is like a hangman's noose. All of this will be a memory, but a victorious one. I'll still be here with this woman who I want as my wife."

Athena stared at him openmouthed. He took the opportunity then to plant a kiss that even took his breath away.

"Surprise!"

Athena stood on the porch with Cicely and Thelma not believing what she saw. She couldn't believe her eyes.

"What the heck are you doing here?" Athena cried and laughed. "It's so good to see all of you."

"Your letters were killing us. We *had* to see this place. Then the kids sounded so adorable. And your boss sounds yummy," Naomi raved.

"Where is he?" Denise asked. She offered Cicely and Thelma a small wave.

"Right here." Collin stepped from the truck with their suitcases.

Denise hooted. "Oh, no, I thought you were just the driver."

"I figured that."

Athena could barely see. Her eyes filled with tears of joy. Her sorors had come. She'd missed them so much. She turned to Collin. "How did you know they were coming?"

"I arranged it." Asia stepped out from the car.

Athena screamed and ran toward her twin. Now she really was crying. But the heaviness of the day slipped off. She had friendships to celebrate.

Quickly, she introduced everyone. The men joined them, too. The only missing person was Lorraine. Athena had heard through Clarissa that Lorraine did it out of jealousy. She had feelings for Collin that were never reciprocated. Maybe one day, she could deal with hearing her name. But she couldn't say that she was terribly upset that she chose to leave with Dominique.

"Let's go inside." Athena led them into the house.

After they finished exploring, she had to get the information.

"Now how did all of this happen?" Athena asked Asia.

"I contacted Collin and told him that I wanted to surprise you. He picked this date. Actually it was supposed to be tomorrow, but that flight got canceled. Then I told the others we should come to see you, but didn't tell them I was talking to Collin."

"Wait a minute, where is Sara?" Athena looked around the room to make sure that she didn't miss her.

"Very pregnant. She's beside herself that she can't be here."

Athena clapped her hands. "Oh, I'm going to have a niece."

"Or nephew." Asia gave a thumbs-up.

Denise nudged Athena. "So heard you have big news."

"What?" Athena looked around the room. "News about me?"

"Our news," Collin explained.

Cicely brought a black box from off the dining table and handed it to Collin.

He lowered himself to one knee.

The living room was quiet, except for Athena's sniffing.

"Give her a tissue, please," Denise prompted. She snatched a tissue for herself, too.

"Athena, you are my earth that has kept me grounded and humble. You are my wind that has lifted me higher with your love. You are my fire that has lit a path through the storm. Will you marry me?"

"Always and forever."

When you can't trust anyone, the only thing
you can do is trust your heart….

Essence Bestselling Author

GWYNNE FORSTER

*P*RIVATE LIVES

Following a bitter divorce, Allison Sawyer seeks seclusion at
a rustic mountain retreat. Though attracted to her neighbor,
Brock Lightner, she's wary and keeps her distance. Intrigued
by Allison, Brock wonders who she's running from—and how
he can convince her he'll do anything to protect her.

"A delightful book romance lovers will enjoy."
—Romantic Times BOOKreviews
on *Love Me or Leave Me*

Coming the first week of March 2009
wherever books are sold.

Are they ready for their close-up?

Essence **Bestselling Author**

LINDA HUDSON-SMITH

Romancing THE
RUNWAY

It seems as if supermodels Kennedy and Xavier have it all—hot careers and each other. But crazed schedules, constant media attention and unruly paparazzi threaten their fragile new relationship. Can their searing physical attraction and soul-deep connection be enough to guarantee a picture-perfect ending?

Coming the first week of March 2009
wherever books are sold.

KIMANI™
ROMANCE

REQUEST YOUR FREE BOOKS!

2 FREE NOVELS
PLUS 2 FREE GIFTS!

KIMANI™
ROMANCE

Love's ultimate destination!

YES! Please send me 2 FREE Kimani™ Romance novels and my 2 FREE gifts (gifts are worth about $10). After receiving them, if I don't wish to receive any more books, I can return the shipping statement marked "cancel." If I don't cancel, I will receive 4 brand-new novels every month and be billed just $4.69 per book in the U.S. or $5.24 per book in Canada, plus 25¢ shipping and handling per book and applicable taxes, if any*. That's a savings of over 20% off the cover price! I understand that accepting the 2 free books and gifts places me under no obligation to buy anything. I can always return a shipment and cancel at any time. Even if I never buy another book from Kimani Press, the two free books and gifts are mine to keep forever.

168 XDN EF2D   368 XDN EF3T

Name	(PLEASE PRINT)	
Address		Apt. #
City	State/Prov.	Zip/Postal Code

Signature (if under 18, a parent or guardian must sign)

Mail to The Reader Service:
IN U.S.A.: P.O. Box 1867, Buffalo, NY 14240-1867
IN CANADA: P.O. Box 609, Fort Erie, Ontario L2A 5X3

Not valid to current subscribers of Kimani Romance books.

Want to try two free books from another line?
Call 1-800-873-8635 or visit www.morefreebooks.com.

* Terms and prices subject to change without notice. N.Y. residents add applicable sales tax. Canadian residents will be charged applicable provincial taxes and GST. Offer not valid in Quebec. This offer is limited to one order per household. All orders subject to approval. Credit or debit balances in a customer's account(s) may be offset by any other outstanding balance owed by or to the customer. Please allow 4 to 6 weeks for delivery. Offer available while quantities last.

Your Privacy: Kimani Press is committed to protecting your privacy. Our Privacy Policy is available online at www.eHarlequin.com or upon request from the Reader Service. From time to time we make our lists of customers available to reputable third parties who may have a product or service of interest to you. If you would prefer we not share your name and address, please check here. ☐

KROM08R